The night was silky dark and q~~~~ apart from the endless shrill song of the cicadas. The sky above her head was a vault of black velvet, the stars closer than she had ever seen them before.

"Tired?" he asked.

"A little," she admitted.

He reached for the robe she had discarded earlier, and wrapped it around her.

"In that case..." Taking her hand, he led her toward the hot tub.

It was screened from the house and terrace by a waist-high semicircular stone wall, but the front was open to what in daylight would be a pleasant view over the gardens.

As they approached, Perdita could hear the faint bubbling sound of water and see wisps of steam rising from the surface. A nearby alcove held a neat pile of towels.

Slipping the robe from her shoulders, he said, "This is what you need."

A broad seat made a horseshoe around the tub, and when she had descended the steps, she sat down, submerged up to her shoulders.

The gentle, erotic swirl of hot water around her weary limbs felt lovely, and she was just starting to relax when Jared inquired, "Mind if I join you?"

Her breath caught in her throat.

LEE WILKINSON attended an all-girls school, where her teachers, often finding her daydreaming, declared that she "lived inside her own head," and that is still largely true today. Until her marriage she had a variety of jobs, including PA to a departmental manager and modeling swimsuits and underwear.

As an only child and avid reader from an early age, she began writing when she and her husband and their two children moved to Derbyshire. She started with short stories and magazine serials before going on to write romances for Harlequin® Books.

Lee is a lover of animals. After losing Kelly, her adored German shepherd, she now has a rescue dog named Thorn, who looks like a pit bull and acts like a big softy, apart from when the postman calls. Then he has to be restrained; otherwise he goes berserk and shreds the mail.

Traveling has always been one of Lee's main pleasures, and after crossing Australia and America in a motor home and traveling around the world on two separate occasions, she still periodically suffers from itchy feet.

She enjoys walking and cooking, log fires and red wine, music and the theater, and still much prefers books to television—both reading and writing them.

CLAIMING HIS WEDDING NIGHT
LEE WILKINSON

~ WEDLOCKED ~

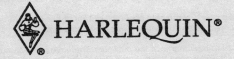

HARLEQUIN®

TORONTO • NEW YORK • LONDON
AMSTERDAM • PARIS • SYDNEY • HAMBURG
STOCKHOLM • ATHENS • TOKYO • MILAN • MADRID
PRAGUE • WARSAW • BUDAPEST • AUCKLAND

Recycling programs
for this product may
not exist in your area.

ISBN-13: 978-0-373-52758-8

CLAIMING HIS WEDDING NIGHT

First North American Publication 2010.

Copyright © 2010 by Lee Wilkinson.

This edition published by arrangement with Harlequin Books S.A.

For questions and comments about the quality of this book
please contact us at *Customer_eCare@Harlequin.ca*.

www.eHarlequin.com

Printed in U.S.A.

CLAIMING HIS
WEDDING NIGHT

CHAPTER ONE

IT WAS a lovely early June day. After a miserably cold spring, a cloudless blue sky hailed the start of summer in the city.

The dust and heat and the oppressive air that trapped and held the exhaust fumes hadn't yet built up. Instead, a light balmy breeze played hide and seek, fluttering flags and awnings, and giving London the air of being *en fête*.

In spite of the financial problems that at present beset JB Electronics, the bright sunshine lifted Perdita Boyd's spirits and put a spring in her step as she walked along Piccadilly.

Tall and slender, with a natural grace of movement, even in a business suit, her hair in a no-nonsense coil, she turned male heads.

Considering herself to be somewhat nondescript, with eyes of palest turquoise and hair the bleached gold of ripe corn, she would have been surprised had she known what an impact she made.

Even the elderly, and somewhat crusty, bank manager she had been to see earlier that morning, whilst refusing to give JB Electronics a loan, had smiled at her and sighed for his lost youth.

After leaving the bank, attempting to gather herself and regain some shred of optimism, she had called in at the nursing home where her father was recovering from recent heart surgery.

John Boyd had been sitting by the long windows that looked out over the well-kept grounds.

He was a tall, nice-looking man of just turned fifty five, with a good head of thick grey-blond hair and a slight gap between his top middle two front teeth that gave him a boyish appearance.

As she'd crossed the room to kiss him, he had queried, 'No luck, I take it?'

Sitting down opposite, she shook her head. 'I'm afraid not. While the bank manager was sympathetic, he was also adamant that they could offer neither a loan nor a bigger overdraft.'

John sighed. 'Well, as the Silicon Valley set-up is in an even bigger mess than we are, that means we've no alternative but to negotiate with Salingers.'

'It won't be easy. They're a tough lot. They have us over a barrel and they know it.

'Even so, we can't afford to let them have the controlling interest if we can possibly help it. We need to keep it down to no more than forty-five per cent of the shares.'

'I'll do my best.'

'Go up to fifty per cent if you *have* to. When are you going to see them?'

'I'm going to their Baker Street offices first thing tomorrow morning.'

'That's good, we've no time to spare. Who will you be seeing?'

'I've an appointment to see a Mr Calhoun, one of their top men.'

'Yes, I've heard of him. He's a tough nut to crack, by all accounts.'

Wanting to take the worried look off her father's face, Perdita hastily changed the subject. 'Oh, by the way, Sally mentioned that she'd like to pop in later, if that's all right with you?'

'It's fine by me.'

'She said something about getting her own back.'

He grinned. 'She has a pocket chess set, and the last game we played, I beat her.'

Then seriously, 'I take it she's looking after you all right?'

'Can you doubt it?'

'Not really. Sometimes I wonder how we ever managed without her.'

When their previous housekeeper had left to get married, Sally Eastwood, an attractive English widow of forty-five, home from the States after her American husband died, had taken the post.

Hard-working and sunny-natured, in the ensuing six months Sally had proved to be an absolute gem. Born and bred in Lancashire, she had soon become part of the family.

A tap at the door announced the lunchtime trolley.

'Well, I'd better be on my way,' Perdita said, stooping to kiss her father's cheek.

'The best of luck for tomorrow, lass,' he said, touching her hand.

Then, obviously trying to hide his anxiety, 'I don't hold out much hope of reaching an agreement straight away though, heaven knows, we need to.'

'If there does seem to be any chance of an agreement, will you need to consult Elmer first?'

'No. He's given me carte blanche to do whatever is necessary to save the company.' Then, quickly, 'When you've been to see Calhoun, you'll let me know how things are going?'

'Of course.'

She and her father had always been very close, and Perdita knew how much he hated being hors de combat at this crucial time.

Her face soft and concerned, she went on, 'I know you'd much rather you or Martin were doing this negotiating, but—'

'That's just where you're wrong, lass,' he broke in firmly.

'You've got what it takes, and I think your chances of pulling it off are appreciably better than mine. Or Martin's, for that matter.'

Martin, who lived with them in London and ran the Technical Information side of the company, was the only son of Elmer Judson, John's American business partner. As well as being the apple of Elmer's eye, Martin was also a lifelong favourite of John's, taking the place of the son he had never had.

So for him to say that *she* had a better chance of pulling it off than either himself or Martin was high praise indeed.

Pleased by his vote of confidence, Perdita had walked back through the park. Feeling hungry, and lured by the sight of an empty bench in the sun, she had sat down to eat the sandwiches that Sally had packed for her, before continuing back to work.

Once back at the company's Calder Street offices, she would grab a quick cup of coffee before starting the afternoon's work.

While her father was convalescing, and Martin was in Japan on urgent business, Perdita was to all intents and purposes, running the firm.

Whilst coping with the extra pressure of work, she was struggling to make the final preparations for her wedding to Martin, which was now only six weeks away.

He had bought her a beautiful diamond solitaire, and their engagement had been officially announced early that spring, bringing in its wake an absolute whirl of activity.

But things were finally coming together. The church and the caterers had been booked, her dress was being made by Claude Rodine, and yesterday, after consulting her father, she had made the final arrangements for a marquee to be erected on the lawn of their home in Mecklen Square.

Now, all that still remained to be done was...

Her train of thought was suddenly and violently derailed by the sight of a tall, well-built man with dark hair leaving a taxi that had just drawn up outside Piccadilly's Arundel Hotel.

Brought up short by the shock, Perdita stopped dead in her tracks, scarcely aware that another pedestrian following on her heels had to sidestep abruptly to avoid walking into her.

No! It couldn't be! It just couldn't! She *had* to be mistaken.

But, as the man paid the driver and turned to head for the hotel entrance, she knew that she had made no mistake. She could have picked out that clear-cut, handsome profile from a million others.

'Oh, dear God,' she breathed.

Jared.

Jared who, after all this time, still had the power to stop her heart.

He had reached the entrance when, as if sensing her presence, he paused and looked back.

Always in the past, on entering even a crowded room, he had known precisely where she was without having to look.

Now, as he turned his head and their eyes met, she felt as if she had been kicked in the solar plexus.

While she stood and gazed at him, rooted to the spot, he smiled slowly, mirthlessly.

That smile made her blood run cold. The moment she had dreaded, and felt in the depths of her being was inevitable, had arrived.

Adrenalin surged through her and, though she knew it was hopeless, knew he wouldn't let her go so easily, she turned blindly to run.

As he moved to intercept her headlong flight, a taxi that had pulled up alongside her to drop a fare started to draw away.

Dragging open the door, she scrambled in anyhow and, weak-kneed and trembling, her heart thumping like a sledge-hammer, sank onto the seat.

'Where to?' the driver asked laconically, swinging out into the traffic stream.

Though all her attention was fixed on the man standing gazing after them, instinctively cautious, she answered, 'The top end of Gower Street.'

For the entire length of Piccadilly the traffic was heavy and slow-moving and, as the taxi crawled along, the blood drumming in her ears, she kept glancing over her shoulder.

There was no sign of any pursuit but, even so, it was a few minutes before her heart stopped pounding and she could breathe properly again.

She was safe.

At least for the time being. But suppose he had finally managed to track her down? Suppose he knew exactly where to find her?

She shuddered at the possibility.

Still, if he *had*, she thought, rallying a little, what could he possibly *do?*

But, recalling his smile, cold chills began to run up and down her spine, and she was forced to admit that her attempt at bravado had failed miserably.

The Jared she had fallen in love with had been passionate and caring, with a strong sense of justice and fair play. Even then, however, he had been quite capable of setting aside conventional or so-called 'ethical' standards and being ruthless.

She shuddered again as the word *ruthless* brought a return of her previous panic.

Gritting her teeth, she told herself firmly that she mustn't lose her head. It would all depend on *why* Jared was in London. It might have nothing to do with her.

He might be over from the States on a business trip of some kind. Or perhaps he was here on holiday? His mother had been born in Chelsea and he had always had a soft spot for London.

But neither option seemed logical. The Arundel was the

haunt of the rich, and the last time she had had news of him he had been virtually penniless.

Of course he might *not* be staying at the Arundel, but just lunching there.

She took a deep steadying breath. And it was quite possible that seeing each other had been merely an unlucky chance. A case of her being in the wrong place at the wrong time.

If she hadn't been passing the hotel at that precise moment she would no doubt have remained in blissful ignorance of Jared's presence in town.

But, even more important, *he* wouldn't have known for sure that she was living here.

Three years ago, when she and her father had returned home from California, John had taken every precaution to keep their exact whereabouts a secret.

He had changed both the name and address of the company, bought a different house in a different location, and had their home telephone number listed as ex-directory.

In short, he had made it as difficult as he could for Jared to find them.

Difficult, but not impossible…

'This OK?' The driver's voice cut through her jumbled thoughts.

'Oh, yes…fine, thanks.'

Gathering herself, she paid him, added a tip and climbed out.

As he drove away, she started to walk on. It was about a quarter of a mile to the Calder Street offices, but she had been afraid to be dropped any closer in case Jared had managed to get the number of the taxi.

Her legs still felt shaky, and she wished Martin was here in London rather than in Japan.

Whilst she had struggled to forget Jared and all the pain his perfidy had caused, Martin had been her anchor, her safe harbour, and she missed his reassuring presence.

He was an attractive man, tall and sturdily built, with fair hair and cornflower-blue eyes. A man she felt sure would make a good husband and father.

Even so, it had taken three years of patient, undemanding devotion on his part to finally get her to accept his proposal of marriage.

Now she would be glad when the wedding was over and they were man and wife. She would feel safer. Be—almost—able to believe that she had finally managed to escape from the past.

But though Martin had admitted that he had first fallen madly in love with her when she was just seventeen, she knew she would never again feel the kind of passionate love she had felt for Jared.

Nor did she want to. It was too traumatic. It had brought nothing but bitter disillusionment and heartbreak.

Or so she told herself.

In truth, it was simply that having once given her heart she had nothing left to give, just a void where her heart should have been.

All she felt for Martin was gratitude for his unfailing support, and an almost sisterly affection.

But, even so, he still wanted her and she was satisfied that she could make him happy and, while he would never rock her world, neither would he cause her pain.

When John and Elmer were told the news the two men had been highly delighted.

'I've always known how he felt about you,' Elmer had told her, 'so I wasn't surprised when he decided to follow you to England. I'm just pleased that his tenacity has finally paid off. There's no one I'd sooner have for a daughter-in-law.'

While her father had said gladly, 'I can't tell you how pleased I am that you've finally decided Martin's the man for you. Dangerfield couldn't be trusted and would never have amounted to anything; I was beginning to think you'd never get over him.'

Only Perdita knew in her heart of hearts that she *hadn't* got over Jared, and she never really would. Hadn't she spent the last three years trying?

Reaching the glass and concrete tower block that housed JB's suite of offices, Perdita exchanged greetings with the security guard before taking the lift up to the second floor.

In the outer office, Helen, their attractive blonde secretary-cum-PA, glanced up from her computer to ask hopefully, 'Did you have any luck?'

Perdita shook her head. 'Unfortunately not.'

Helen, who'd been with them for the past three years, sighed. 'How did your father take it?'

'Very well, really. I think he'd resigned himself.'

'So now your only hope is Salingers?'

'I'm afraid so.'

'Then you'll just have to charm their Mr Calhoun.'

'I didn't manage to charm the bank manager,' Perdita said wryly.

Helen grinned. 'Perhaps you just weren't his type.'

Once in her own office, Perdita disposed of her handbag and hung up her jacket before sitting down at her desk.

But, though she had a great deal of administrative work to get through, try as she might, she couldn't concentrate. Jared was once again occupying her thoughts to the exclusion of all else.

She found herself rerunning the little scene outside the Arundel over and over again in her mind, wondering how it might have ended if the taxi hadn't been there at just the right moment.

But it was, she told herself sternly, so she must avoid dwelling on other possibilities and try to dismiss all thoughts of Jared from her mind.

Only that was easier said than done.

His dark face and the memories it brought flooding back

refused to be banished and by four-thirty she had achieved very little in the way of work.

She had just decided to give up and go home when the phone rang and Helen told her, 'Mr Calhoun's secretary would like to speak to you. She's on the other line.'

'Thanks.'

Fearing the worst, Perdita picked up the receiver and said, 'Perdita Boyd speaking.'

A woman's voice, sounding cool and efficient, responded, 'Miss Boyd, I have a message for you. Unfortunately, Mr Calhoun has been forced to cancel your appointment.'

Knowing only too well how urgently they needed the lifeline Salingers had appeared to be holding out, Perdita's heart sank like a stone.

Trying to keep her voice level, she asked, 'Can you tell me the reason?'

'Mr Calhoun needs to fly to the States tomorrow morning,' the secretary told her crisply. 'The only way he can find time to see you is if you can meet him at the airport and talk to him over breakfast.'

Unable to hide her eagerness, Perdita agreed, 'Yes. Yes, I can do that.'

'In that case, if you'll give me your home address I'll arrange for a car to pick you up at six-thirty tomorrow morning.'

Perdita gave her the address and thanked her before ringing off.

Feeling like a condemned woman who had been granted a last-minute reprieve, she phoned her father to tell him of the change of venue.

Then, having pulled on her jacket, she collected her bag and made her way through to the outer office, where Helen was just preparing to leave.

'Problems?' the other woman enquired, her face sympathetic.

'Just a change of plan, thank the Lord.'

Perdita explained briefly what that change of plan involved, adding, 'So it could have been worse. I only hope he's not in too much of a hurry to really listen to me.'

'Amen to that. Well, if you want to get off, I'll lock up.'

'Thanks. See you sometime tomorrow.'

The phone call had temporarily driven thoughts of Jared from the forefront of Perdita's mind but, as she started to walk home, memories of the past came flooding back in a relentless tide.

She had been born in the States, but her American mother had died soon after and her distraught father had taken her back to England with him.

After she'd left school, in order that she should see something of the country of her birth, her father had taken her over to California for a prolonged visit.

Elmer, who owned a large house near Silicon Valley, had insisted that the pair of them stay there with himself and Martin.

Perdita had been in San Jose for only a matter of days when she and Jared had met at a party. She had fallen in love with him at first sight—love like a deep, fast-flowing river that she had plunged straight into without stopping to ask herself if she might drown.

Right from the start, it had been like sharing a self with him. They had completed each other, filled each other's lives and hearts. She had thought of them as soulmates.

But in the end that whole concept of closeness, of belonging together, had proved to be just an illusion. A lie.

He was tall, dark and handsome—a hackneyed phrase but a true description—a charismatic man who had always attracted the opposite sex like buddleia attracted butterflies.

But, with eyes only for her, he had never seemed to notice them. Even so, in the early days of their relationship she had had to struggle hard to hide her jealousy when one of them had touched him or smiled at him.

When one day she had admitted as much, he had kissed her and said, 'There's no need to be jealous, my love. I'm a one woman man, and *you're* that woman. There'll never be anyone else for me.'

Wanting desperately to believe him, she had almost succeeded, until that awful night in Las Vegas and the nightmare that had followed.

She remembered his tight-lipped silence when her father—who was still recovering from his recent heart attack—had called him a swine and a heartless Casanova, and peremptorily ordered him out of the house in San Jose.

Remembered only too well how Elmer Judson and Martin, both big, heavily built men, had advanced on him threateningly when he had refused to leave without her.

But, even then, Jared hadn't said what she had dreaded him saying, the one thing that would have shocked her father and stopped the other two men in their tracks.

Perhaps he had expected *her* to say it.

But she hadn't.

And a melee had ensued.

Jared was young and fit and more than able to defend himself, she knew, but, with a bruised cheek and a split lip, he had never once hit back.

Even so, it had taken the combined efforts of both Elmer and Martin to throw him out, while she had stood like a statue, tears spilling out of her eyes, and watched, ignoring his repeated pleas of, 'Come with me, Perdita.'

The final blow had been when her father had reneged on a promise to help finance Dangerfield Software through a crisis.

That last minute failure to honour an agreement that had been previously signed and settled had forced Jared into near bankruptcy.

Even then he hadn't stopped trying to get her back. After weeks of unanswered letters and phone calls, he had appeared in the Silicon Valley offices of Judson Boyd and asked to speak to her in private.

Still raw and bleeding from his betrayal, and knowing only too well that there was nothing he could say that would alter things, she had shaken her head and asked him to leave.

Standing his ground, he had once again sworn he was innocent and accused her of refusing to listen to him, of lack of trust, of never really loving him.

The latter had brought stinging tears to her eyes. But, fighting against the surge of emotion, and flanked by her father and Martin, she had told him that he was wasting his time, that she never wanted to see him again.

When he would have argued further, he had been 'escorted' from the premises.

The last few bitter words they had exchanged had been over the phone.

When she had felt able to, she had rung him to repeat that everything was over between them, that she wanted to be free of him, and that she and her father were leaving the States for good.

It was then he had warned, 'Don't think I'm letting you go so easily. Sooner or later I'll find you, wherever you are.'

Now, just thinking about it, made her shiver.

But, though it was still so vivid in her mind, it had been almost three years ago. Surely after this length of time he would have moved on?

In all probability he was married. When they had once talked about their future together, he had said he wanted children so he might even have started a family.

She could only hope that his life was now settled and stable, and that he had forgotten the past.

But suppose he hadn't? Suppose he was here in London because of her? Suppose he had finally managed to track her down?

Becoming aware that her unhappy thoughts had gone full

circle, she brought herself up short. It was high time she stopped thinking about Jared and started to concentrate on tomorrow, and what was bound to be the most important meeting of her life.

The next morning, after a virtually sleepless night when she had spent hours lying awake trying not to think about the past, Perdita was up at five-thirty.

Her head throbbed dully and she felt like death warmed up—an expression of her father's that until that minute she hadn't fully understood.

Glancing at herself in the bathroom mirror, she grimaced. Just when she had wanted to look her best and radiate an air of efficiency and confidence, she looked like something the cat had dragged in.

Oh, well, she would just have to see what ravages a spot of make-up could hide.

Showered and dressed in a smart charcoal-grey business suit, small chunky gold hoops in her neat lobes, her blonde hair taken up into a fashionable knot, she checked her appearance in the cheval glass in her bedroom.

Her skin was flawless, so normally she needed very little in the way of cosmetics. Now, just a light coat of foundation hid the slight shadows beneath her eyes, while a pale lip gloss and a hint of blusher bestowed a healthy glow.

Her brows and lashes were naturally darker than her hair and needed only a touch of mascara to define them even more.

After a critical survey could find no real fault with her appearance, she picked up her bag and headed for the stairs, just as Sally's voice called, 'The car's here now.'

'Coming.'

The housekeeper, who had insisted on getting up to see her off, was waiting in the hall. With a quick hug, she said, 'I only hope everything goes well.'

Then, looking oddly flustered, she added, 'I really *do* have your best interests at heart.'

Returning the hug, Perdita said, 'Thanks. I'll give you a ring and let you know how it goes.'

A little awkwardly, Sally told her, 'I won't be home. I promised I'd pop over and have breakfast with your dad. I thought it might help to take his mind off things. Or, at the very least, give him someone to talk to. I hope you don't mind?'

Touched by her concern, Perdita said warmly, 'Of course I don't mind. On the contrary, it sounds like a great idea.'

Outside, it was another lovely sunny day, the air as cool and sparkling as champagne. At that time in the morning the square was still quiet and in the central gardens dew sparkled on the grass and the beds of early summer tulips.

A dark blue limousine was drawn up by the kerb with a uniformed chauffeur waiting to open the door. As she crossed the pavement, he said a cheerful, 'Good morning, miss.'

Perdita returned his greeting and, trying not to feel like someone about to try and successfully negotiate a minefield, climbed in and fastened her seat belt.

Traffic was very heavy and the journey seemed to be taking so long that she began to worry about being late. If she missed this appointment, the consequences would be disastrous.

On tenterhooks, she breathed a cautious sigh of relief when they finally reached the airport environs and a few minutes later drew up in an area she didn't immediately recognize.

A smartly dressed sandy-haired young man was waiting for them.

Before turning to lead the way into the terminal building, he greeted her with a smile and a courteous, 'Good morning, Miss Boyd. My name's Richard Dow and I work for Salingers.

'I'm pleased you were able to make it in time,' he went on as they crossed the VIP lounge. 'The traffic seems to get worse.'

To her surprise, Perdita found herself escorted through

heavy glass doors and out onto the tarmac apron where a private executive jet stood close by, its immaculate white and blue paintwork gleaming in the bright sunshine.

As though sensing her surprise, Richard Dow said, 'Didn't Mr Calhoun's secretary mention that Salingers executives usually have breakfast on the plane?'

'No. No, she didn't… Not that it matters,' Perdita added hastily. 'It's just that I was expecting…' The words tailed off as they reached the plane and she was ushered up the steps.

A white-coated steward was waiting in the doorway to welcome her aboard. 'Good morning, Miss Boyd. My name is Henry. If you'd like to follow me?'

Short and nimble, his black slicked-back hair gleaming, he led the way through to a small but luxuriously furnished lounge where a table was set for breakfast with damask linen, crystal glasses, a bottle of Krug on ice and a jug of freshly squeezed orange juice.

Pulling out a chair, he deftly settled her at the table. 'If you would like a glass of champagne and orange juice while you're waiting? Or a coffee, perhaps?'

Her head still aching and intent on keeping a clear brain, Perdita said, 'A cup of coffee would be nice, thank you, Henry.'

Having assembled brown sugar and cream, the steward took a glass jug of coffee from a hotplate and filled her cup.

Then, indicating a nearby bell push, 'If you require anything further, Miss Boyd, just ring for me.'

She thanked him and, silent-footed, he disappeared through a sliding door in the bulkhead.

Relaxing a little now that she was sure the meeting was going ahead, she sipped her coffee and surveyed the quiet luxury that surrounded her.

There were two soft leather armchairs, several bookcases, a comprehensive in-flight entertainment centre and a small leather-topped desk.

Salingers did their top men proud, she thought, taking in the sumptuous carpeting and the two striking paintings by Joshua Lorens that she recognized as originals rather than prints.

With this kind of money at their fingertips, they should have no trouble bailing out half a dozen struggling companies. So all she had to do was persuade them that buying into JB Electronics would be a good investment in the long run...

Deep in thought about the coming meeting, it was a moment or two before she realized that the plane was moving, taxiing slowly across the apron.

Perdita had half risen to ring for the steward before it occurred to her that the area was getting busy and the pilot was probably just moving up to accommodate another plane.

Sinking back into her seat, she picked up her cup and was about to take a sip when the bulkhead door slid aside and a well dressed man walked in. A tall, broad-shouldered, handsome man with crisp dark hair and silvery-grey eyes.

Every trace of colour draining from her face, leaving the blusher standing out like a circus clown's make-up, she set down the cup with a clatter, splashing coffee into the saucer.

Staring at him, wide-eyed and speechless, she wondered wildly if all the strain of her father's heart surgery and the company's financial problems, coupled with the little scene outside the Arundel, had affected her brain and she was imagining the whole thing.

'Hello, Perdita,' he said softly.

Though she hadn't heard him speak for three years, she would have known that deep, attractive voice anywhere. It could have called her from the grave.

'What are you doing here?' she asked hoarsely.

'Standing in for Sean Calhoun.' Jared's tone was neutral, almost pleasant, but his grey eyes were as cold as the Atlantic in winter. 'So, if you want to save your father's company, you'll have to negotiate with me.'

CHAPTER TWO

PERDITA jumped to her feet and, her heart racing, scarcely able to breathe, stammered, 'I…I don't understand. Do you mean you work for Salingers?'

'Not exactly.'

'Then what is this?' she demanded raggedly. 'Some kind of joke?'

'No, not at all.'

'I don't believe you. If you don't work for Salingers—'

'I don't actually *work* for them, but you could say I'm here on their behalf,' he broke in smoothly.

She shook her head. 'No, no… Even if it means waiting, I'd prefer to deal with Mr Calhoun. I don't want to talk to you.'

'I'm afraid you have no option. As I said before, if you want to save your father's company you'll have to negotiate with me.'

Clutching her bag, she moved a step or two towards the door, desperate to escape. But, tall and dark and dangerous, he was effectively blocking her way.

Hearing the panic in her own voice, she said, 'I want to leave.'

'Giving up so easily?' he taunted.

'Not at all,' she denied jerkily. 'I'll talk to Salingers. Explain to them. Ask to see someone else.'

'I'm afraid it won't be any use.'

'Why won't it?'

'Because I own the company.'

'*You* own Salingers?' she said through dry lips.

'That's right.' Smiling a little at her shocked face, he went on, 'So I suggest you sit down again and we'll talk over breakfast, as planned.'

Shaking her head, she insisted, 'No, I want to go now. There's absolutely no point in staying. I know perfectly well that you've no intention of helping.'

'That's where you're wrong. I'm quite sure we could come to some kind of agreement that would satisfy both of us.'

It was a trick, and she knew it.

'No, I don't trust you.'

'You can't afford not to,' he pointed out laconically. 'Without my help JB will go under, and you know it.'

It was the truth. But she couldn't believe that he really intended to help.

There was a series of slight bumps, and part of her mind registered that the plane was still moving away from the terminal building.

Getting more anxious by the moment, she repeated hoarsely, 'I want to leave.'

When he made no attempt to move, taking her courage by the scruff of the neck, she advanced towards him purposefully. 'If you don't let me pass, I'll be forced to scream.'

'Dear me,' he said mildly. 'We can't have that. Though Henry may *look* a little like a gigolo, he's really quite sensitive and easily upset.'

Knowing he was laughing at her, Perdita gritted her teeth. 'I *mean* it.'

Without moving, he queried, 'How is your father's health these days?'

'What?'

'I understand he's recently undergone delicate heart surgery. Can he afford any further stress?'

When, white to the lips, she merely stood and stared at him, he went on, 'So suppose you take the sensible option and stay and talk to me?'

'It wouldn't do any good.'

'Let's have breakfast and see, shall we?'

While he was speaking there was a knock, the door slid aside and the steward put his head round. 'Excuse me, sir, but the Captain asked me to let you know we have a slot and will be taking off in a minute or so.'

'Thanks, Henry.'

As the man disappeared, Jared turned to Perdita. 'It looks like breakfast will have to wait until we're airborne.'

Airborne.

Her paralyzed brain clicking into gear, she tried to push past him. 'I must leave before it takes off. I must!' she cried frantically.

Catching her wrist, not hurting, but keeping her where she was, he said, 'I'm afraid you've left it much too late.'

'No, no, you have to let me get out! I can't possibly go with you!'

'Once again, you have no option. The outer door's secured and we're at the top of the runway. We need to be seated for take off.'

As she strove to come to terms with this latest development, Jared urged her into the small forward cabin, where the steward was already buckled into one of the jump seats.

Recognizing the futility of arguing, she submitted to being pressed into one of the seats. Then Jared fastened her belt and tightened it, before taking his place beside her.

A few moments later the plane began to move down the runway, gathering speed.

Take-off seemed quick and effortless and, as soon as they had climbed steeply to the required height and levelled out, the steward disappeared through a curtained doorway.

Perdita, who had sat like a statue, her thoughts in chaos, burst out, 'I don't know what you hope to achieve by this—'

Jared put a finger to her lips, stopping her breath and sending a shiver running through her. 'I'll tell you what I hope to achieve as soon as we've had breakfast, but in the meantime we don't want to upset Henry.'

He unfastened their seat belts and shepherded her through to the lounge area.

'I really don't want to eat,' she protested. 'In the circumstances, I'd prefer to know just what you're playing at.'

His voice holding a quiet authority, he said, 'I'll be happy to tell you, once breakfast is over.'

When, biting her lip, she was once again seated at the table, he stood for a moment or two looking down at her before taking the chair opposite.

He was dressed in oatmeal-coloured trousers and a well-cut lightweight jacket, with a navy-blue silk shirt and a matching tie loosened at the neck. His crisp dark hair was parted on the left and cut and styled conventionally.

But even as the thought struck her, she knew there was nothing remotely conventional about Jared.

Unable to look away, she found herself staring at his handsome face. He was the same, yet not the same. Any trace of the younger, carefree Jared she had first met was gone. This man was altogether harder, tougher, with a mature width of shoulder and lines of pain etched beside his mouth.

Meeting those brilliant eyes and glimpsing a cold purpose in them, she shuddered and tore her gaze away just as the steward wheeled in a breakfast trolley loaded with several silver dishes.

He was about to serve them when Jared said briskly, 'Thank you, Henry. We'll help ourselves. But perhaps you'd be good enough to fetch Miss Boyd a clean cup and saucer?'

'Certainly, sir.' The dirty crockery was whisked away and immediately replaced by fresh. Then, with a slight inclination of his gleaming head, the steward withdrew silently.

'Coffee?' Jared enquired politely.

Subduing a sudden desire to laugh hysterically, Perdita answered with equal politeness, 'Please.'

He filled both their cups before lifting the lids of the various dishes and enquiring, 'What's it to be? Bacon and eggs? Sausages? Kidneys? Mushrooms?'

'Nothing, thank you. I couldn't eat a thing,' she told him stiltedly.

'Try. You're too thin as it is.' Looking at her set face, he added, 'Starving yourself isn't going to solve anything and, if I remember rightly, you used to enjoy bacon and eggs.'

She sat in tight-lipped silence while he served her with a generous amount of crisp bacon and fluffy scrambled eggs before helping himself to the same.

Then, his eyes fixed on her face, he waited.

His willpower proved to be stronger than hers—as it always had been—and finally she gave in and picked up her knife and fork.

He waited until she put the first forkful of food into her mouth before starting on his own.

Once Perdita began to eat, in spite of all the trauma, she found that her normal healthy appetite was back and she cleared her plate.

Jared made no comment, but he swapped the plate for a clean one and put the toast-rack within easy reach.

When she sat unmoving, he helped himself to some toast and spread butter and marmalade on it in a leisurely fashion.

Seeing he had no intention whatsoever of saying anything until he was good and ready, she threw in the towel and followed suit.

She had just taken her first bite when, with a glance from

beneath long dark lashes, he remarked slyly, 'The last time we had breakfast together like this, we were in Las Vegas.'

Her eyes on her plate, she kept chewing in silence.

'But perhaps you don't remember?'

She remembered only too well.

All her life Perdita had been cosseted and cared for, guarded as well as any chaperoned miss from the Edwardian era.

Naturally quiet and a little shy, and loving her father as much as he loved her, it had never occurred to her to feel caged and stifled by so much care and affection.

That was, not until she met Jared and wanted enough freedom to spread her wings.

At first everything had gone well. Her father had been prepared to both like and respect him until Martin had mentioned that Jared had a bad reputation with regard to women.

Suddenly waking up to the fact that his beloved daughter might be in danger, John had ordered her to give, 'that young Dangerfield' a wide berth.

She would certainly have rebelled but, as her father had recently suffered his first heart attack and his doctors had warned against worries or stress of any kind, she had, outwardly at least, complied.

For several months she and Jared had been forced to meet in secret, snatched moments together that had left both of them dissatisfied and bitterly unhappy.

He had begged her to marry him and present her father with a fait accompli, but she had been afraid to chance it while his recovery was still uncertain.

Then, while Elmer was away in New York, John had had to go into Mardale, a Los Angeles hospital, for a week of special and extensive tests.

Perdita had made up her mind that if the results were good and showed that her father was more or less recovered, she would tell him the truth.

When the time had come for John to go to Los Angeles, he had refused to let her accompany him, saying there was no point in her simply hanging around a hospital all that time. She would be much better off at home.

'After all,' he had added, 'it's not as if you'll be on your own. Martin will be there.'

Truth to tell, she had been pleased to stay behind. It had given her a few precious days to be with Jared.

That sudden taste of freedom had gone to both their heads, and when he had suggested a trip to Las Vegas she had eagerly agreed.

All the tawdry glitter of that city in the desert had seemed to be right and romantic, and she had been blissfully happy to be with the man she loved, with no idea how it was all going to end…

Feeling suddenly chilled through and through, Perdita snapped off the thought and brought her mind back to the present.

What had made him mention Las Vegas? she wondered. She didn't for a moment believe it was just an idle remark. Jared never did or said anything without a good reason.

Which meant it would only be playing into his hands to ask.

Holding on to her facade of composure as best she could, she ate her toast in silence while she waited for him to finish his coffee.

As soon as he had, she gathered her courage and said, 'Now perhaps you'll be kind enough to tell me what all this is about?'

'All what?' he asked innocently.

'This…whole thing.'

'You mean our meeting? But surely you—'

'Don't try to play games with me,' she broke in angrily. 'This must have been planned right from the start.'

'That's quite true,' he admitted.

'So it was *you* who made sure Salingers approached my

father to suggest they might have a solution to all his company's financial problems?'

'Right.'

'Why?'

'Why do you think?'

'You planned to wait until the very last minute and then withdraw your offer of help.'

'Wrong.'

'I don't believe you… Your intention was to watch JB Electronics go down.'

'Now why should I want to do that?'

'Revenge.'

'Ah… I can't deny revenge is sweet.'

'But after three years! Surely you've moved on? Forgotten the past?'

'Have you?'

Watching all the colour drain from her face, he said, 'It wouldn't appear so.'

'Even if things aren't forgotten,' she argued desperately, 'surely they cease to hurt so much? Anger cools…'

'I'm not so sure about that.'

Though his tone was quiet, almost pleasant, she began to shiver.

Seeing that slight betraying movement, he smiled a little. 'Though I *am* sure of one thing. As the old saying goes, "Revenge is a dish best served cold".'

'So I was right,' she choked. 'You *are* planning to stand by and gloat while Dad's company goes under?'

'You're quite mistaken.'

He sounded as if he meant it and, brought up short, she gazed at him, perplexed.

'Then what *are* you planning? There has to be some reason for…' The words tailed off as a frightening thought struck her.

'For you being here?' He smiled coldly. 'Oh, yes, there's a reason. More than one, in fact.'

With a boldness she was far from feeling, she demanded, 'Well, are you going to tell me? Or would you prefer me to guess?'

'What is your guess?' he asked interestedly.

Her throat dry, she said, 'That I was right about you wanting revenge... I just got the wrong person.'

When he made no attempt to deny it, she swallowed convulsively. 'So this whole thing was set up just to lure me to the airport and on to the plane... Well, it can't possibly work!'

'It's worked so far,' he pointed out.

'But it's kidnapping! And, in case you haven't realized, kidnapping is against the law.'

Her attempt at sarcasm only made him smile.

'How can you call it kidnapping? You got on the plane of your own free will.'

'But when I wanted to get off, you wouldn't allow me to.'

'My dear Perdita, surely you realize that people can't just get off a plane and start wandering about on the runway.'

Realizing it was fruitless to keep arguing, she relapsed into silence.

If luring her here *was* so he could extract some kind of revenge—and he had failed to deny her accusation—how far did he mean to go? Was it his intention simply to scare her? Give her an uncomfortable couple of hours before letting her go?

Or could he have something altogether more sinister in mind? No, surely not.

She had accused him of kidnapping without seriously believing it. All the indications were that he was now a wealthy and respectable businessman with a position to maintain. Not some kind of criminal.

But, whatever, it would do no good to let him see how rattled she was.

Taking a deep breath, she said, 'Very well, you've won so far. But now what? If I don't get back to the office soon they'll wonder where I've got to, and if Dad doesn't hear from me before too long he'll start to worry.'

'There's no reason why you shouldn't phone him. And the office too, if it comes to that.'

'You won't try to stop me?'

'Certainly not. After all,' he added sardonically as she reached for her bag, 'we can't have your father worrying about you.'

His words echoing in her head, she froze. What could she possibly tell her father that wouldn't worry him half to death?

Watching her, well aware of her dilemma, Jared suggested, 'Perhaps it would make more sense to talk business first? That way, if you can convince me that the company is worth saving, you'll have something positive to report.'

Though she deeply mistrusted him and was convinced that any discussion would be futile, seeing nothing else for it, she agreed, 'Very well.'

'Before we start, it might be an idea to move to somewhere more comfortable.'

Rising to his feet, he pulled back her chair and seated her in one of the soft leather armchairs, before summoning the steward to clear away the remains of breakfast.

As soon as Henry had cleared the table and whisked away the trolley, Jared moved to join her.

Settling himself opposite, he stretched his long legs negligently and, his eyes on her face, waited.

When she said nothing, he invited, a shade mockingly, 'Go ahead.'

But the reasoned arguments and the facts to support them that she had previously rehearsed had fled and, faced with a mental block, she hesitated.

Apparently appreciating her difficulty, he suggested, 'Why not pretend I'm Sean Calhoun and tell me why I should buy into JB Electronics?'

His words provided a key to the block. Taking a deep breath, she began by explaining what had caused the company's present difficulties before going on to outline exactly what was needed to restore the balance and make them really profitable once more.

He listened without interrupting, his almond eyes fixed on her face. Extraordinary, handsome eyes, long-lashed and heavy-lidded, with jet-black pupils and silvery-grey irises.

Eyes that in the past had, depending on his mood, made her think of cold winter moonlight, or the dangerous gleam of rapiers, or the brilliance of summer lightning...

Dragging her recalcitrant thoughts back to the task in hand, she went on a shade unsteadily, 'We have several excellent new projects in the pipeline which, once they're properly funded, should be winners. In other words, the company is well worth saving.'

'Eloquently put,' he applauded. 'But presumably your bank is unwilling to either provide a loan or extend your overdraft?'

Convinced that he already knew she'd tried and failed, and was relishing it, she said tightly, 'That's right.'

'As JB Electronics is an Anglo-American concern, I take it that the present problems aren't confined to the UK, but affect the company as a whole?'

'Yes,' she admitted with a sigh. Even Elmer's big house in San Jose—the house that she and her father had stayed in when they were in the States—was very heavily mortgaged.

'So, to get a rough idea of how things stand overall, how much does the company owe the banks?'

She told him.

'And how much are you in debt to your suppliers?'

When she had told him that too, he asked, 'What about your workforce?'

'Up until now we've managed to pay them.'

'How?'

Wondering exactly what he was getting at, she sat in tight-lipped silence.

When she failed to answer, he remarked smoothly, 'I understand that your house in Mecklen Square is mortgaged up to the hilt?'

She had opened her mouth to deny it when the obvious truth of his statement hit her like a blow over the heart.

It explained so many things. Things John hadn't wanted to discuss or had hedged over.

As she stared at Jared in horror, he said, 'I see you didn't know.'

Why on earth hadn't her father told her? she wondered despairingly.

But even as she posed the question, she knew the answer. Only too aware that she had enough worries and unwilling to spoil her forthcoming wedding, he had deliberately kept it from her.

'How remiss of your father to send you to negotiate without telling you the full facts,' Jared remarked silkily. 'It leaves you at a disadvantage.'

Angered by his obvious satisfaction, she demanded sharply, 'How come you know so much?'

'Past mistakes have convinced me that it's preferable to negotiate from a position of strength, so I made it my business to find out.'

'Well, bully for you,' she said bitterly.

'Now we come to the question of assets…'

It took a moment or two to gather herself before she admitted, 'As no doubt you already know, at present we have no viable assets.'

'Hmm…' He ran long, lean fingers over his smooth, freshly shaven chin while he sat and studied her heart-shaped face in silence.

She was still as lovely as ever, he thought, with her pure bone structure and pale blonde hair, her flawless complexion and those fascinating eyes, the clear greeny-blue of turquoise.

But it was more than the high cheekbones, the wide passionate mouth and the cleft in her softly rounded chin that made her beautiful. It was the character in her face, the warmth and individuality.

As the silence lengthened, well aware that this was torture by hope, teeth clenched together, she waited, determined to show no sign of impatience.

Only when her nerves were stretched almost to breaking point did he stir himself and say briskly, 'Right. If my auditors' report agrees with what you've just told me, I'm prepared to buy into JB Electronics and provide as much money as it takes to put it back on its feet.'

She released the breath she had been unconsciously holding. It sounded like the answer to all their prayers, but Jared was an unlikely, not to say *unbelievable*, saviour and she recalled one of her father's pet sayings. 'If it sounds too good to be true, it probably is.'

She took a deep steadying breath. 'And, presumably, for that kind of outlay, you'd want to take over and run the entire company?'

'No.'

'Then what would you want?'

'Fifty-one per cent of the shares.'

'That would give you overall control.'

'Nominally. Though I would be quite happy to leave the running of the company in your father's hands.'

Given that kind of reassurance, had it been anyone other

than Jared, she felt sure she could have agreed, with her father's blessing.

After all, what choice did they have?

But, with all that had happened in the past, none of them would trust Jared an inch.

'I could never agree to fifty-one per cent,' she said through stiff lips.

'So what would you agree to? Forty-five, fifty, if it proved to be really necessary?'

'Yes,' she admitted. 'But certainly not more.'

'Pity. I could save JB. Make it profitable again. But of course it's your choice.'

A choice between the rock and the whirlpool. A choice she couldn't possibly make alone.

Her greeny-blue eyes clouded with worry, she said, 'I'll have to talk to my father.'

'But you don't think he'd trust me enough to agree to fifty one per cent?'

'He'd be a fool if he did.'

Jared laughed as though genuinely amused. 'Well, I'm pleased to see you haven't lost all your spirit. It'll make things more interesting.'

She was wondering what he meant by that cryptic remark when he reached over and took her hand. 'In view of the fact that in the past you and I—'

The shock of his touch made her stomach clench and, pulling her hand free, she cried jerkily, 'The past's dead and done with.'

'Now that's where you're wrong. What's happened in the past makes us what we are today.'

The fact that she knew it to be true only served to make her distrust him even more.

'But, as I was saying, taking into account that in the past you and I were lovers, I might be prepared to negotiate.'

Just for a split second hope flickered into life, then almost immediately died. Why should he negotiate when he so assuredly held the whip hand?

Showing he never missed a thing, he remarked with a slight smile, 'You don't appear to be overjoyed at the prospect.'

'I don't believe for a minute that you mean to budge,' she said flatly.

'You'll never know for sure until you try.'

As she began to shake her head, he advised evenly, 'In view of what the outcome might be if you refuse, perhaps you should take a minute to think about it.'

Reminded of the dread consequences, she bit her lip. Then admitting defeat, she said heavily, 'I don't have any option.'

'Exactly.'

His voice holding the merest hint of triumph, he added, 'As any negotiations are going to take time, I've a suggestion to make...'

Eyes on his face, she waited.

'And it's this, that you speak to your father and tell him that, though things are looking hopeful, there's still a long way to go.

'However, while the negotiations are under way, as a gesture of goodwill, Salingers will put in place a financial package that will pay wages, hold off your creditors and keep things ticking over.'

Had the offer been made by anyone other than Jared she would have regarded it as a lifeline, but, as it was, she strongly suspected that in reality it was a carefully baited trap.

She was even more convinced when, looking at her from beneath long thick lashes, he added, 'It might be as well to keep my name out of it and let your father think that you're dealing with Calhoun.'

'But that would give him a totally false picture,' she protested.

Jared lifted broad shoulders in a slight shrug. 'It's up to you, of course. If you think he can stand the additional stress and worry, tell him the truth by all means...'

As she reached for her phone, he added casually, 'There's just one more thing. Tell him that I have to be in the States for the next ten days or so, and that I've invited you to join me there while further discussions take place—'

'I don't know what you expect to gain by this,' she burst out, 'but if you think for one minute that I'd go anywhere with you, you're mad!'

He sighed theatrically.

'Oh, yes, I know,' she cried, her voice bitter, 'I don't have much option.'

'In view of the fact that we're already over the Atlantic, you don't have *any* option.'

As she bit her lip, he added, 'Now, as time is flying, your father must be getting anxious to hear from you...'

He would be, she knew, and over the past weeks his hypertension and the amount of stress he was under had proved to be a big concern for his doctors.

But what was she to say to him?

A few seconds' thought convinced her that it would be far too risky to tell him the truth. He was bound to find out sooner or later, of course. But for the moment at least, she would go along with Jared's scenario, while she tried to put in place some kind of damage limitation.

Taking a deep breath, she strove to steady herself. Her father knew her well and, as the news she was about to give him would appear to be as good as anyone had dared hope, she mustn't allow him to pick up any signs of distress.

As she brought up the number of the nursing home, Jared rose to his feet and, showing the kind of supreme confidence that made her grit her teeth, said, 'I'll leave you to it,' and disappeared into the forward cabin.

At the first ring, her father's voice asked eagerly, 'Perdita?'

'Yes.'

'I was just starting to get worried. How are things going? Any hope of saving the company?'

Trying to sound positive, she said, 'Yes, I think there might be.'

'So what does Calhoun want?'

She hesitated, then went along with it. 'He started off by asking for fifty-one per cent of the shares.'

'Just as I thought,' John said grimly.

'But when I told him you wouldn't agree to that, he said he might be willing to negotiate.'

'The trouble is, negotiations like that could take weeks, and we just don't have the money to keep going in the meantime.'

'He's offered us a way round the problem.' Perdita explained about the immediate injection of cash.

She heard her father's sigh of relief before he remarked, 'In the circumstances, that's extremely generous. I mean, Salingers must know they have us right where they want us.'

'Yes,' she agreed. 'But of course it could well prove to be a two-edged sword, as it will effectively put us in debt to them.'

As soon as the words were spoken, she bit her lip, realizing just how worried and despondent she must have sounded.

'Well, in the circumstances, we haven't much choice,' John said practically. 'And I'm only too relieved and thankful that you've done so well. I always knew I could rely on you.'

When, pierced to the heart by such undeserved praise, she remained silent, he added, 'Look at it this way; we've got a stay of execution while the negotiations take place, so there's still a chance.'

Trying to sound cheerful, she agreed, 'Of course.'

CHAPTER THREE

'SO WHERE are you now?' John asked. 'On your way back to the office?'

After a moment's panic, Perdita lied, 'No. I'm still at the airport.'

'But Mr Calhoun's gone, I imagine?'

'No, not yet.'

'I thought he was planning to leave early?'

'Yes, he was, originally.'

Then, trying to sound calm and matter-of-fact, she went on, 'But things have changed. You see he's due to be in the States for the next ten days or so, which means the face-to-face negotiations he prefers would be held up...'

Her voice not quite as steady as she would have liked, she went on, 'So he's suggested that I go with him, as his guest.'

'To New York, presumably?'

Though she didn't know for sure, it seemed easier to answer, 'Yes.'

'And you've agreed, of course?'

'Well, I...'

'Don't worry about the office,' John said eagerly. 'Apart from anything else, a few days in New York might prove to be a nice little break for you.

'I understand Salingers have a couple of hospitality suites at their Fifth Avenue headquarters that are on a par with the Plaza.'

When she didn't immediately answer, he repeated, 'Don't worry about this end. I'm quite sure Helen can hold the fort until Martin comes back. It's much more important to get these negotiations over and done with successfully.

'I presume Salingers have their own plane?'

'Yes. I've just had breakfast on board their executive jet.' It was such a relief to be able to speak the truth that she added, 'And pretty luxurious it is, too.'

She heard her father's chuckle before he remarked, 'Well, at least you'll be travelling in style.'

Then, as she hesitated, wondering just what to tell him, he queried, 'I take it Salingers' car will be running you back home to pick up your passport and some clothes?'

His words sent her into a spin. *Of course! She would need a passport!* Why hadn't she thought of that straight away?

Because Jared's presence, plus all the stress and worry, had effectively scattered her wits.

But why hadn't Jared himself realized that she couldn't land in the States without a passport?

She felt a little thrill of satisfaction and triumph. Whatever he'd been hoping to achieve, his plan had backfired.

'Are you still there?' John enquired.

'Yes, yes, I'm still here.'

'I was saying, I assume that Salingers' car will be running you back home to pick up some clothes and your passport?'

'Yes, that's right.' Then, afraid her father might suggest that she popped in to see him, she added hastily, 'But I'll be very pushed for time.'

'I don't doubt it. Well, have a safe journey, lass, and let me know when you get there.'

'I will,' she promised. 'Take care of yourself.'

She ended the call, feeling oddly shaky. It had gone much

better than she had dared hope. Though she dreaded to think what the future held, for the moment, at least, her father had sounded more relaxed than he'd been for some time.

She tried to hold on to that comforting thought.

A quick calculation told her that it should be early evening in Tokyo but, feeling very alone and vulnerable, she hesitated to phone Martin in case she weakened and poured out all her worries and fears.

After all, there was nothing he could do, so what was the point of upsetting him?

The same applied to Helen.

When the other woman answered the phone, Perdita steadied herself and reeled off a brief version of the same story she had told her father.

'It sounds hopeful,' Helen commented. 'And, whatever you do, don't worry about this end. I can cope. By the way, have you talked to Martin yet?'

'I had so much on my mind last night, I forgot to recharge my phone,' Perdita said, glad of an excuse, 'so my battery's low. Will you ring him for me and explain that I'm going to the States as Mr Calhoun's guest? Tell him I'll be in touch later.'

'Of course. Well, the best of luck.'

'Thanks. I may need it.'

Aware of how heartfelt that must have sounded, Perdita sighed and dropped the phone back into her shoulderbag.

Barely a moment later the door slid aside and Jared strode in, giving the impression he always gave of having abundant energy and vitality.

Just the sight of him jolted her, making her heart pick up speed and her breath catch in her throat.

'You've spoken to your father?' he enquired with the air of a polite host.

'Yes.'

'I do hope you managed to reassure him?'

The false concern grated and she said coldly, 'Why should you care?'

'Oddly enough, I would prefer not to have his death on my conscience.'

'Then can I suggest that trying to kidnap his daughter is going the wrong way about it.'

'I don't know why you insist on referring to it as kidnapping. You're simply accompanying me as my guest, albeit a somewhat unwilling one.'

'Guests, even "somewhat unwilling ones", usually have some clothes with them.'

'Don't worry,' he said airily. 'From past experience I know what a beautiful body you have, and I much prefer you without clothes.'

Watching the hot colour pour into her cheeks, he added, 'And there's sure to be plenty of nice warm sunshine in California.'

'California!' she exclaimed. 'Why California?'

'Because I still live there.'

Just those five little words made her feel as though she were in a lift that had dropped too fast.

'After a refuelling stop in Boston,' he continued evenly, 'we'll be flying on to San Francisco…'

Then, seeing her dismay, 'Where did you think we were going?'

'I…I didn't know for sure. I suppose I'd presumed it would be Salingers' headquarters in New York.'

'Is that what you told your father?'

'It's the conclusion he jumped to.'

Then, unable to keep the satisfaction out of her voice, she went on, 'Not that it makes a great deal of difference. Wherever we're heading for, I won't be able to get off the plane.'

'Really?' he queried interestedly. 'Why not?'

Triumphantly, she pointed out, 'Because I can't land in the States without my passport.' Sweetly, she added, 'And I'm afraid I don't have it with me. Which leaves you with a bit of a problem.'

'Not really.'

'What do you mean, not really? What are you intending to do? Try and smuggle me in?'

'My dear Perdita—' there was mockery in his voice '—do credit me with a little sense.'

He felt in his jacket pocket. 'Your passport.'

Looking at the document he was flourishing, she said, 'I can't deny it's a passport, but it's certainly not mine. Mine is at home in my bureau.'

'That's just where you're wrong.' He opened the pages to show her a picture of herself.

As she gazed at it in disbelief, he slipped it back into his pocket.

Finding her voice, she accused, 'You've gone so far as to have a *fake* passport made!'

'Not at all. It's the genuine article.'

'It can't be!'

'I assure you it is.'

As she struggled to take in the implications of that, he added, 'And, in the hold, there's a suitcase carefully packed with everything you should need for at least the next couple of weeks.'

Common sense insisted that it couldn't be so, that he just *had* to be lying. Yet she knew he wasn't. Somehow he'd managed to acquire both her passport and a case full of clothes.

But how?

Even if he'd known exactly where she lived and where to find her things, he could hardly have walked in and taken them himself. Someone must have helped him. It was the only explanation that made sense.

But who?

A moment's thought convinced Perdita that there was only one person who *could* have helped him, and that was Sally.

Sally, whom they'd grown fond of. Sally who, instead of being merely a housekeeper, had become like part of the family.

No, no, she couldn't believe that Sally would do such a thing!

But even as she tried to refute the charge, Perdita recalled that morning and how flustered the other woman had looked as she'd insisted, 'I really *do* have your best interests at heart'.

Jared, who had been watching her expressive face, smiled. 'I didn't think it would take you too long to work it out.'

Gritting her teeth, she asked, 'How on earth did you get Sally to do your dirty work for you?'

'She doesn't regard it in that light. She sincerely believes that what she did is for the best.'

'I don't believe you.'

'Then you should.'

Bogged down, unable to think straight, Perdita said helplessly, 'I don't understand how you managed it. How you got to know her…'

'As luck would have it, we first met when she and her husband lived in California. When I discovered she was your housekeeper, I asked for her help.

'Initially she refused, saying it would be quite wrong and disloyal. But, in the end, after I'd told her everything, she agreed. She thought that she was helping to put things right.'

'What things?'

'Past mistakes.'

Perdita let that go and attacked from another angle. 'How did you know where we lived?'

'As soon as I was on my feet again, I set about tracing you. It wasn't easy, but eventually I discovered where you lived and also that your father's business was in trouble.

'I thought out a plan that I knew might, or might not, work. Discovering that I knew your housekeeper was an unexpected bonus, and when she finally, and I must admit reluctantly, agreed to help, I went ahead with that plan.'

Studying her face, and noting how pale and exhausted she looked, how *disillusioned*, Jared sighed. 'Try not to blame Sally. While I gather she has little time for Martin, she's extremely fond of you and your father.'

'And you think that makes everything all right?'

Avoiding a direct answer, he said, 'I would be sorry if you turned against her. She genuinely believes that everything she's done is for the best.'

'You mean that's what you've managed to brainwash her into believing!'

'Not at all. She's an intelligent woman and a moral one and before she would agree to my suggestion I had to convince her it was justified.'

'And how did you do that?'

'I simply told her the truth.'

'And she believed you?'

'I'm pleased to say she showed a great deal more faith in me than you did.'

Hearing the bitterness in his voice, Perdita bit her lip. If Jared was still so caught up in the past, it didn't look as if he had married and moved on as she had first hoped...

There was a knock and the door slid aside. 'Excuse me, sir,' Henry said, 'but Captain Benedict would like a word with you.'

'Will you tell him I'll be with him in just a moment or two.'

'Certainly, sir.'

Jared turned to Perdita and said, with a show of concern that wrenched at her heart, 'You look absolutely shattered.'

'I didn't get a great deal of sleep last night,' she told him stiffly.

'I would judge that to be an understatement. But, if you'd like to stretch out, there's a perfectly good bedroom along there.'

'A bedroom?' she echoed.

'Come and take a look.'

He led her to the far end of the lounge area, where another

door opened into a small but nicely fitted bedroom with an en suite shower-room.

Indicating a comfortable-looking bed with built-in cabinets either side, he said, 'As we've still got a long journey ahead of us, I suggest that you get a couple of hours' sleep before lunch.'

The sight of the bed brought back memories of another bed in Las Vegas. A bed where Jared's tanned and muscular body had looked so devastatingly male against the pink silk sheets and frilled pillowcases.

She took an involuntary step backwards and heard his soft chuckle.

Proving how well he could read her mind, he said, 'Don't worry, I wasn't thinking of joining you.'

Though he spoke with light mockery, she saw his silvery eyes darken almost to charcoal and a little lick of flame flicker in their depths.

She remembered that look well, and though in the past she had welcomed it, seeing it now made her blood run cold with apprehension.

'Unless you *want* me to, that is?'

'No, I *don't* want you to!' she choked.

He sighed. 'Pity… Ah, well, I'll go and get some work done and leave you to it.'

Sketching an ironic salute, he closed the door.

When she had hung her suit over a chair and taken off her shoes, Perdita pushed the lightweight duvet aside and stretched out on the bed. She felt weary, body and soul, but so uptight that she had no hope of actually sleeping.

She had gone along with Jared's suggestion merely to buy herself some time alone. Some time to think. To try and decide just what he had in mind. What he hoped to gain.

The sudden hunger she had glimpsed in his eyes had frightened her half to death. At that moment she had realized that, though he might hate her, he still wanted her.

But everything else had changed. She no longer loved him, and she was about to marry someone else.

But would that be enough to keep her safe?

Yes, surely it would.

Jared wasn't a man who would dream of using force… As the thought went through her mind, her heavy eyelids closed…

She was awakened by a discreet knock at the door.

Sitting bolt upright in alarm, momentarily confused and unsure of just where she was, she asked hoarsely, 'Who is it?'

'It's Henry, miss. Mr Dangerfield thought you might like a cup of coffee…'

Feeling more than a little dazed, she answered, 'Oh, yes… Yes, thank you,' and pulled the duvet up around her.

The steward came in with a tray of coffee and put it down carefully on the bedside cabinet before continuing, 'He asked me to say that we'll be landing at Logan Airport in about twenty minutes to refuel.'

She thanked him and, with a slight inclination of his gleaming head, the steward departed, closing the door quietly behind him.

Her hair was coming down and, after a fruitless attempt to repair the damage, Perdita reached to pour the coffee.

With so much on her mind, so many worries about Jared's motives and intentions she hadn't expected to sleep. But, if they were almost at Boston, she must have slept for several hours.

Refreshed by the drink, she washed her face and hands in the shower-room and took the pins from what remained of her chignon, only to realize that her comb and make-up were still in her bag, which she had left in the lounge.

At the same instant there was a knock at the bedroom door and Jared's voice called, 'Sorry to rush you, but in a minute or so we'll need to take our positions for landing.'

'Coming,' she answered in a muffled voice and, twisting her long corn-coloured hair into a knot, secured it as best she could.

Then, quickly, she pulled on her skirt and jacket and, feeling as if she'd been dragged through a hedge backwards, made her way to the lounge, where Jared was waiting for her.

She was vexed to find he looked fresh and virile and supremely confident, with not a hair out of place. Once again, just the sight of him made every nerve in her body tighten and her heart start to beat faster.

His eyes on her face, he enquired with smooth urbanity, 'Feel any better?'

Knowing her hair was a mess and her nose was shiny, and conscious of being even more at a disadvantage, she answered stiltedly, 'Yes, thank you.'

'Then let's get ready for landing.'

When they touched down at Boston, knowing her father would be waiting for her call, Perdita reached for her phone.

She had been debating what to tell him. Should she admit that this was just a refuelling stop and that they would be flying on to San Francisco? Or let him go on believing they were going to Salingers' headquarters in New York?

She was still struggling to decide when Jared slanted her a sideways glance and enquired, 'Have you made up your mind whether to let him think we're at JFK, or admit we're at Boston?'

'I don't know what to tell him,' she admitted helplessly. 'What do you think—?' She broke off, vexed that she had actually asked his advice.

Seeing her bite her lip, and realizing the cause, Jared smiled a little before suggesting, 'Wouldn't it be simpler, and cause him less worry, to let him go on believing that you're in New York?'

'But suppose he tries to contact me there?'

'I'll talk to the office and put them in the picture, make sure they channel any calls that go there straight through to California.'

Somewhat cheered by that assurance, and knowing she'd need to tread carefully, she went ahead and called her father.

'Hi, Dad, we've just landed.'

'Good journey?'

'Very good. You know where to find me if necessary, but I'll keep in touch.'

'Have you spoken to Martin yet?'

'Not directly,' she hedged. 'But Helen was going to let him know what was happening.'

'Well, I'd better let you go. I know the next few days are going to be tough, certainly no holiday, but if you get the chance try to have a little fun.'

'I will,' she promised. 'And I'll ring you as soon as I've anything to report. In the meantime, take care of yourself.'

Their goodbyes said, she ended the call and, still afraid to talk to Martin, dropped the phone back into her bag.

'Everything OK?' Jared queried.

'It seems to be. Though I really *hate* having to lie to him.'

'Surely it's better to…shall we say *mislead* him, rather than worry him with the truth?'

'I suppose so,' she agreed with a sigh.

The refuelling was completed quickly and efficiently and in a relatively short space of time they were airborne again.

When they'd reached the required height and levelled out, Jared unfastened their seat belts and they returned to the lounge.

After his comment about it being better to mislead her father than worry him with the truth, he had relapsed into a thoughtful silence.

Now, sitting opposite Perdita, he studied her face before remarking, 'What with your father's heart problems, the company's financial difficulties and the added workload, the last few months must have proved quite a strain.'

Wondering what he was leading up to, she agreed warily, 'Yes. Why do you ask?'

Looking at the fleshless angles of her face and the hollows beneath her cheekbones, he observed, 'Because you're thin almost to the point of gauntness, and extremely pale.'

'I'm not wearing any make-up,' she pointed out, her voice defensive.

'You hardly wore any make-up in the past, but I've never seen you look so wan.'

His reference to the past putting a silken noose around her neck, she observed huskily, 'In that case it must have been the Californian sunshine that made all the difference.'

Then, as the steward wheeled in the lunch trolley and began to lay the table, she reached for her bag and said, 'If you don't mind, I'd like to tidy my hair before lunch.'

Jared, who had risen to his feet with his customary good manners, agreed, 'By all means.' As she walked away he added, 'Don't put it up.'

'Martin prefers it up.'

'Martin doesn't happen to be here—' his voice was like steel '—and *I* prefer it down.'

Once in front of the shower-room mirror, she applied make-up with an unusually lavish hand before tugging a comb through her hair and pinning it into an extra-neat coil.

A little scared of Jared's reaction to her defiance, she had hoped that when she returned the steward would still be there. But he had completed his task and gone.

Rising to his feet once more, Jared looked at the prim coil through narrowed eyes. As he moved towards her, she unconsciously took a step backwards but he seated her at the table and pushed in her chair without a word being spoken.

She was just breathing a sigh of relief when he slid a hand beneath her chin and tilted her head back so that she got a glimpse of his dark face, intriguingly inverted.

Then it blurred out of focus as he bent and kissed her mouth, a hard, ruthless kiss that forced her head back and her lips apart.

Though she knew that kiss was meant to be punitive, a punishment for defying him, it made every nerve in her body come alive.

She made a little sound in her throat and the pressure eased and gentled.

When he finally freed her lips, his hand remained on her throat for a moment or two, stroking up and down, making her swallow convulsively.

As she sat quite still, trembling in every limb, he removed the pins and dropped them into his jacket pocket. Then, as the gleaming mass tumbled around her shoulders, he ran his fingers through the soft tangle of perfumed curls before stooping to bury his face in them.

Holding her breath, she recalled with a stab of pain that he had always been fascinated by her hair, referring to the pale brightness of the silken strands as trapped sunshine.

Not until he straightened and moved to take his own seat opposite did she drag air into her lungs like someone who had stayed under water for too long.

Lifting the lid from a steaming dish, he filled two plates with a generous helping of prawn pilaf before pouring them each a glass of Chablis.

Lunch proved to be a silent meal. Jared appeared to be deep in thought and Perdita was battling against a host of worries and fears, her mind full of unanswered questions.

When the steward had cleared away, they took their coffee and went to sit in the armchairs.

The silence grew oppressive and Perdita was trying to find something to say when, out of the blue, Jared asked, 'Why are you thinking of marrying Judson? Is it just to please your father?'

'No, it isn't. And I'm not just *thinking* of marrying him. I *am* marrying him. All the arrangements have been made.'

'Arrangements can be cancelled.'

'I've no intention of cancelling them. I *want* to marry Martin.'

'If it's not to please your father, *why* do you want to marry him? Don't tell me you love him.'

'I *do* love him,' she insisted.

Clearly unmoved, Jared said, 'I don't believe a word of it.'

'How can you possibly know whether or not I love him?' she demanded angrily.

'I'd lay a pound to a penny that your feelings for him are no more than lukewarm, so you might as well admit it.'

'If you really want to know, I'm mad about him!'

Jared threw back his head and laughed.

'How dare you laugh at me!' she cried, made almost incoherent by anger.

'That kind of out-and-out lie is enough to make a cat laugh,' he told her.

'It happens to be the truth,' she insisted, with what dignity she could muster.

After a moment he pursued, 'If you're so mad about him, why has it taken you all this time to say yes?'

As she struggled to find an answer, Jared changed tack to ask, 'Tell me, is he a good lover?'

Thrown by the question, she flared, 'That's none of your business.'

'But perhaps you don't sleep together?' he suggested smoothly.

After a momentary hesitation, she informed him coldly, 'Certainly we do.'

'Where?'

'What do you mean, where?'

'As you both live in the same house as your father,' Jared explained patiently, 'it must be a little awkward.'

'Not at all.'

'So you share a room?'

'Of course.' Only when the words were out did she see the trap he'd lured her into.

'That's funny,' he said meditatively. 'Sally seemed to think you have separate rooms.'

As Perdita floundered, at a loss for words, Jared asked sardonically, 'No comment?'

Rallying, she said, 'Even if we do have separate rooms, it doesn't mean we don't love one another.'

'I quite believe he loves you,' Jared said. 'Or at least what passes for love,' he added, contempt in his voice. 'But if you love him as much as you say you do, it strikes me as peculiar that, in this day and age, you don't share a room.'

As she opened her mouth to protest, he went on, 'And it strikes me as even more peculiar that you felt it necessary to lie about it.'

'I might have lied about us actually sharing a room, but we certainly sleep together.'

'Sally seems to think you don't.'

'Really?' Perdita said bitterly, 'What else does Sally "seem to think"?'

'Since you ask, she seems to think that, though Judson might be mad about you, your feelings towards him are more platonic than passionate.'

'And I suppose she knows all about feelings?'

'Why shouldn't she? I understand that she and her husband loved each other very much, and she was shattered when he died.

'She told me that it's only since becoming your housekeeper, and getting to know you and your father, that she's come back to life and started to look forward rather than backwards.'

'Are you telling me she's fallen in love with Dad?'

'Have you never noticed?'

'Now you come to mention it,' Perdita said slowly, 'there's something about her, an added glow, when they're together...'

Then, thoughtfully, 'And though to the best of my knowledge, Dad's never looked at another woman since my mother died, it's possible that he feels the same way about her.'

'What makes you think that?'

'I've noticed he seems to smile more when he's with her, and when she's not there and he talks about her, his face softens and lights up.'

'If they do care for each other, would you mind?'

After some thought, Perdita answered honestly, 'If you'd asked me that yesterday I'd have said no, I'd be only too pleased for them both. But as it is...'

Jared sighed. 'I had hoped you wouldn't hold what she did against her.'

'Whether *I* do or not is beside the point. When Dad knows the truth, surely it'll depend on how *he* feels about it?'

'Does he *have* to know?'

As she hesitated, his tone eminently reasonable, Jared went on, 'Won't what you tell him depend on how the negotiations go?

'I mean if everything turns out well, in view of his heart problems, wouldn't it be safer to keep any unpleasant or worrying details from him?'

'As in, "Least said, soonest mended"?'

'Exactly. Though trite, there's a great deal of sense in some of those old sayings.'

While she recognized that he was trying to protect the woman who'd helped him, there was a lot of truth in what he said.

Another thought struck her. If she agreed to keep any mention of Sally out of it, it might help to bring about the kind of settlement she'd originally been hoping for.

'If I agree, as far as it goes, are you willing to start discussions straight away?'

His voice quietly adamant, he said, 'There's no need to hurry. I plan to stay in the States for at least ten days, so there'll be time enough for business when we reach California.'

It wasn't the answer she wanted but, recognizing the futility of arguing, she let it go.

CHAPTER FOUR

HOPING to get a clearer idea of what she would be facing when they reached the West Coast, Perdita braced herself and began, 'I take it you still live in San Jose?'

'As a matter of fact, I don't.'

'Oh…'

'San Jose had too many unhappy memories.'

Watching his face darken, and feeling the silken noose that was the past tightening around her neck, she asked huskily, 'So where are you living now?'

'Though my main American business interests are still in Silicon Valley, about eighteen months ago I bought a vineyard in the Napa Valley.'

Surprised, she asked, 'How do you find the time to run a vineyard?'

'I don't. I've an excellent manager who takes care of the day-to-day running of the place. You see I've worldwide business interests which necessitate a fair bit of to-ing and fro-ing.

'I've a good right-hand man who would happily do the travelling for me but, until a month or so ago, I've felt the need to keep on the move. However, between each bout of travelling, I've gone back home to relax and unwind.'

Perdita found herself wondering how a man who just three

short years ago had been virtually bankrupt could have made such a staggering recovery.

As though reading her thoughts, he went on, 'Three years ago, when I was on the point of losing everything, my god-father bailed me out.

'He'd been having a tough time himself, then a load of shares he'd considered virtually worthless suddenly came good and, overnight almost, he became a very rich man.

'Less than six months later, when he died, he made me his sole beneficiary, and that's when I started to add to his business empire.'

Though she knew Jared was a businessman born and bred, she had never thought of him as a wine-grower and, a little curious, she asked, 'What made you decide to go into viniculture?'

'My wife has always preferred the countryside and I wanted to have somewhere green and pleasant for her to live. The Napa Valley is beautiful, so it struck me as ideal.'

Jared's casual answer knocked Perdita sideways and she found herself fighting for breath.

When she could drag air into her lungs once more, she asked, 'Then you're married?'

'Yes, I'm married.'

She knew she ought to be glad, but instead that confirmation was like a knife turning in her heart. Momentarily swamped by the pain, she clenched her hands until the oval nails bit deep into her palms.

Then, afraid he might pick up that fierce surge of emotion, she gritted her teeth and struggled hard for at least some degree of composure.

'In view of that,' he went on, 'I've recently got disenchanted with travelling and having my life taken over by business interests.

'I've some very good men working for me. So in the future

I'm planning to delegate a lot of the running of the various companies and just keep a guiding hand on the reins.

'At the same time, however, I wanted something interesting and congenial that would keep me occupied at home, so a vineyard seemed ideal.'

When she felt she could trust her voice, she queried huskily, 'Have you any children?'

'No,' he answered, his voice even. 'Though one day I hope my wife and I will have a family.'

His words only served to increase her anguish, her feeling of utter desolation. Once upon a time *she* had dreamt of being the mother of his children.

That lovely dream had stayed alive, bright and shining, until she had discovered that he couldn't be trusted, then, sadly, painfully, it had died.

So get a grip, she urged herself. All this emotion she was feeling was false. It no longer related to the man himself, but to a dream. An illusion.

The man she had fallen in love with didn't exist. Had never existed, except in her imagination. Even so, it had shaken her rigid to find he had a wife.

She found herself wondering how long he'd been married. Judging by what he'd said about travelling, probably not very long...

Seeing he was watching her, and knowing how well he could pick up what she was thinking and feeling, she took a deep breath and queried, 'What is your vineyard called?'

'Wolf Rock Winery.'

'Is that where we're heading?'

'Yes.'

'Is your wife there now?' She had *had* to ask, and she was relieved that her voice had remained steady.

'No, not at the moment.'

She was just breathing a quick sigh of relief when he added evenly, 'Though she will be soon.'

Perdita was trying to come to terms with that knowledge when a thought occurred to her that made her go hot all over. Suppose Jared had told his wife about *her*?

She desperately hoped not. It would be bad enough having to face the other woman without her knowing about the past and that passionate and, in the end, infinitely bitter relationship.

However, there was nothing she could do to change either the past or the present.

All at once she felt dull and defeated and weary, emotionally drained.

Watching her lovely face, sad now and oddly empty, Jared saw the paleness beneath the make-up, the shadowed eyes and heavy lids, the slight droop of her lips, and felt a strong urge to take her in his arms and hold her close.

But enough anger and resentment still lingered to nullify that sudden surge of sympathy and he merely said, 'In spite of your earlier rest, you still look shattered. Why don't you get another hour or two's sleep before we land at San Francisco?'

Relieved at the thought of being on her own, Perdita rose to her feet, then, recalling what had happened the last time, paused to pick up her bag.

As he had done previously, Jared accompanied her to the bedroom door, but this time he merely said, 'I'll ask Henry to bring you some tea well before we reach our destination.'

When the door closed behind her, moving like a zombie, Perdita slipped off her shoes and once more removed her skirt and jacket before stretching out on the bed.

Though she recognized that the room was at a comfortable temperature she felt chilled, cold inside, and pulled the soft lightness of the duvet over her.

She was on the verge of sleep when her mobile rang.

Reaching for her handbag, she retrieved her phone and mumbled, 'Hello?'

'Dita...?' Martin's voice held a mixture of relief and impatience. 'I've had a lot of trouble getting through to you. What the devil's going on?'

'Didn't Helen explain?'

'It's been very hectic this end and when she couldn't reach me she left a text message which I've only just picked up.

'As I couldn't immediately get through to you, I talked to your father. He confirmed that you'd gone to the States as Calhoun's guest, and that you were staying at Salingers' headquarters in New York.

'I know the negotiations are urgent, but I'm not too happy at the thought of you going off with a man none of us know anything about.'

Perdita was trying to find something reassuring to say when he queried, 'So what's Calhoun like? Is he a married man?'

The question brought a tide of emotion surging back, but she answered as levelly as possible, 'Yes, he's married.'

Then, hoping to divert further questions, she asked quickly, 'So how are things going at your end?'

'As I said, pretty hectic. But, with a little bit of luck, it will have been worth it. Mr Ibaraki is quite happy to...'

For a short while he talked business, then he asked, 'So is Calhoun's wife there?'

'I understand she'll be joining him.' This time, caught unawares, Perdita's voice shook betrayingly.

Martin picked it up at once. 'What's wrong?' he demanded. 'You seem upset.'

'Nothing's wrong,' she lied valiantly. 'I'm just tired. I didn't sleep very well last night, and it's been a long journey.'

Martin, who disliked travelling, agreed, 'Of course. And the time difference doesn't help.'

He sounded sympathetic and, afraid she would burst into tears, Perdita said quickly, 'I'd better go now.'

'Why the hurry?'

'My battery's almost run out. Last night I forgot to charge it, and I haven't got my charger with me.'

'Then I'll keep in touch via Salingers. The best of luck with the negotiations. I hope you get on all right with Calhoun's wife. Things like that can make a difference.'

'Of course,' she agreed hollowly.

'Love you.'

Unable to either answer or stem the emotion any longer, she rang off and dropped the phone back into her bag. Then, curled under the duvet, she gave way to what she recognized as futile tears.

They were still sliding silently down her cheeks when sleep claimed her.

She had no idea how long she'd slept when she was awakened by a knock at the door.

Knowing it would be Henry with the promised tea she sat up, a tangle of pale silky hair tumbling round her shoulders, and trapping the duvet under her arms, called, 'Come in.'

But it was Jared who carried in a tray set with dainty sandwiches and small cakes. 'Tea time,' he said cheerfully.

Every nerve-ending in her body tightening in a sudden panicky confusion, she sat quite still.

When he had put the tray down with care, he settled himself on the edge of the bed, a great deal too close for comfort.

Noticing her frozen expression, he remarked, 'There's no need to look like a scared rabbit. I'm not planning to ravish you.'

'I'm glad about that,' she managed shakily.

His white grin flashed briefly. 'A rabbit with attitude, I see.'

When he moved a little, either by accident or design, his hip pressed against her thigh and she flinched.

Obviously amused by her reaction, he asked, 'So how are you feeling now?'

Even in her own ears she sounded breathless as she answered, 'Much better, thank you.'

Studying her face, where the traces of tears were still evident, he observed, 'Well, you certainly don't look it.' Then, more gently, 'Why the tears?'

Needing an excuse, she told him, 'Martin phoned.'

Sardonically, Jared enquired, 'And does he usually make you cry when he phones?'

'Of course not,' she denied sharply. 'But these circumstances aren't usual...and...and I found I was missing him.'

'You sound like love's young dream,' Jared observed, mockery in his voice.

'And you sound like the heartless devil you are.'

He grinned. 'I must say I prefer you with a dash of spirit.' Then, with a gleam in his eye, 'So what exactly did you tell lover boy?'

Annoyed by the jeer, but unwilling to show it, she answered shortly, 'Not a great deal. He'd already been in touch with Dad, who'd given him all the gen.'

'And?'

'I couldn't see any point in worrying him, so I let him go on believing I was in New York and everything was all right.'

'He wasn't concerned about you flying off with a man you didn't know?'

'As a matter of fact, he was. He made a point of asking if "Mr Calhoun" was married, and if his wife would be with him.'

'And you told him...?'

'I told him yes.'

'That set his mind at rest?'

'I believe so.'

'Perhaps it's just as well. Otherwise, he might have been

donning his shining armour and saddling up his white steed to ride to your rescue.'

'Sarcastic swine,' she muttered.

Jared clicked his tongue reprovingly. 'Now, is that any way for a nicely brought up young lady to talk?'

'If you think—'

He put a finger to her lips, stopping the heated words and effectively silencing her. 'We'd better leave any further invective until later, otherwise our tea will get cold.'

While she fumed helplessly, he filled two china cups with tea, added a little milk and handed her one. Then, putting a selection of small triangular sandwiches on a plate, he set it down within easy reach before drinking his own tea.

In the confined space he was altogether too close, too masculine, and it was a great relief when there was a tap at the door and the steward's voice said, 'I'm sorry to trouble you, sir, but the Captain says could you give him a minute before we land? There's something he'd like to check with you.'

'Tell him I'll be along directly.'

Jared emptied his cup and replaced it on the tray, then, feeling in his pocket, he produced her hairpins. 'Yours, I think. Though I would prefer you *not* to use them.'

Seeing he was waiting for an answer, she muttered, 'Very well.'

He rose to his feet. 'It'll take another half an hour to reach San Francisco, so you have plenty of time to finish your tea and freshen up.'

Their landing at San Francisco International Airport was as smooth as the take-off had been and, in no time at all, it seemed, their baggage had been unloaded and they were descending the aircraft steps.

While Henry followed with their bags, a proprietorial hand

at her waist, Jared escorted Perdita across the hot tarmac to the terminal building.

He was well known to the airport officials and, because they had flown from England to the States and both had dual nationalities, the formalities were over quickly.

Perdita had hoped to claim her own passport but, with an easy movement that took her unawares, Jared slipped it into his pocket.

When she would have argued, he said indulgently, 'Darling, you're such a scatterbrain. It'll be safer with me.'

Her teeth clenched in helpless rage, she had to watch while the little group smiled, before she was shepherded away.

They took the elevator down to the underground parking lot where a white open-topped sports car was waiting in the long-stay section.

Jared unlocked the car and helped Perdita in, while Henry dealt with the luggage.

When their bags were safely stowed in the boot, Jared thanked him and the two men exchanged a few words before the steward turned to walk away.

A few moments later they were leaving the relative gloom of the parking lot and climbing into the dazzling afternoon sunshine. Outside, the cloudless sky was the heavenly blue of lapis lazuli, while the dusty, fume-laden air hung hot and sticky with humidity.

It was three years since Perdita had been on this part of the West Coast but it didn't appear to have changed at all. There were still streams of traffic, massive wayside hoardings and a straggle of unprepossessing glass and concrete buildings.

Right there on her wavelength, Jared remarked, 'It isn't the most exciting scenery in the world, but when I return from my business trips it always makes me feel as if I'm coming home.'

As they nosed out onto the freeway and headed north,

knowing there was no point in sulking, she asked, 'Is it far to the Napa Valley?'

'It's a fair drive, but I think you'll find it's well worth it.'

Already it had been a long journey, and with what he described as a 'fair drive' in front of him she wondered how Jared would cope but, glancing sideways at him, she saw he looked fit and vital and anything but tired.

Noting her glance, he lifted an enquiring brow.

A little thrown and needing something to say, she remarked, 'I'm never quite sure what the time difference is out here.'

'California is in the Pacific Time Zone—eight hours respectively behind Greenwich Mean Time—which means it's already late evening in London.'

When she had adjusted her watch, raising her voice above the wind of their passing and the engine noise, she asked, 'Don't you ever suffer from jet lag?'

'Not as a rule. I've travelled so much over the past couple of years I find it easy to adjust.'

He relapsed into silence and Perdita found herself glad not to have to talk or think.

They had only gone a short distance when, slanting her a glance, Jared saw that her eyes were closed, the long silky lashes curling on her cheeks.

Strands of blonde hair blew around her face and, in spite of the hours she had slept, she still appeared pale and washed out.

She'd always had a delicate, hauntingly fragile beauty, yet he knew quite well that she was anything but weak. She had plenty of spirit and an inner strength that showed itself in the set of her mouth and chin.

But, in spite of that, she looked defenceless and vulnerable. A look that touched his heart.

After a while she stirred and opened her eyes. The air was cooler now and, apart from the whiff of cooking and gasoline from the roadside pull-ins, a great deal fresher. She watched

telegraph lines make long wavy patterns against the deep blue
of the sky and heard the soft phut of insects hitting the wind-
screen before she drifted off again.

The next time she surfaced, the surroundings were altogether more pleasant.

Seeing she was awake, Jared remarked, 'As you can
probably guess, we're in the Valley, in fact, we've just come
through Napa itself. The road we're on now is the St Helena
Highway, the vineyard road.'

Sitting up straighter, Perdita looked around her. As Jared
had said, the Valley was beautiful. Gentle slopes rolled lush
and fertile on either side of the highway, and the balmy air
was redolent of green and growing things.

They reached and passed Yountville, where the road swung
left to skirt the rocky outcrop of the Yountville Hills. Beyond
that, the wide, flat valley, with its steep wooded slopes, began
to narrow a little and they were in the vineyards.

'Wolf Rock is just a mile or two up the road,' Jared told her.

The realization that they were so near brought a sudden
panic. Until now, though she and Jared had been in close
proximity, they hadn't really been alone. Henry had always
been close at hand and they had been on the move.

Being cooped up alone in a house with Jared would be a
different matter.

But surely they wouldn't be *alone*? Even if his wife wasn't
there, he must have staff of some kind to run the place.

Though she made an effort to think positively, it didn't stop
all her previous apprehension returning in force.

It wouldn't have been quite so bad if she'd known exactly
what he was up to, what kind of game he was playing. But his
motives for forcing her to accompany him were still unclear.

As he was married, the notion she had been afraid to acknowledge even to herself—the notion that he might try and
make her go back to him—had obviously been wrong.

So *why* had he planned all this? Why had he held out the hope of saving her father's company and coerced her into coming to the States?

It had to be so he could take some kind of suitable revenge. But what, in his eyes, would be a suitable revenge?

Her father had almost bankrupted him, Elmer and Martin had beaten him up, and she had, in his eyes, at least, failed to either love or trust him.

Of those indictments, two at least were unjust. She *had* loved him. She'd loved him with every fibre of her being. And she *would* have trusted him if he hadn't so lightly betrayed that trust.

But he had sworn he hadn't, sworn he was trustworthy, and an intelligent, down-to-earth woman like Sally had believed him.

That knowledge might well have shaken her, made her doubt his guilt, if she hadn't been there and seen it with her own eyes.

Sighing, still no closer to solving the riddle of *why* he had brought her here, she tried to push all the worries and unanswered questions to the back of her mind.

No doubt she would know the worst soon enough.

She only hoped that for everyone's sake she could save JB Electronics, or at the very least mitigate the final outcome...

Her train of thought came to a halt as Jared turned left and then, after a hundred yards or so, swung right down what appeared to be a private road.

After a short distance they came to a pair of tall black wrought iron gates that stood invitingly open. In an arc above the gates, ornate iron letters read 'Wolf Rock Winery'.

'Home,' Jared said with satisfaction as he drove through the gates.

After a hundred yards or so he drew to a halt in front of a covered, flower-festooned veranda that ran the entire length of a large one-storey house.

Its roof tiles were an orangey-pink and its adobe walls were colour-washed a pale apricot. The two should have clashed, but somehow they appeared to be in complete harmony.

When he had helped her from the car, he took their luggage from the boot, led the way up the veranda steps and opened the door into a large hallway.

Inside, the house, as far as she could see, was open-plan and spacious, with white walls and cool tiled floors.

There appeared to be the minimum of furniture, and she recalled how Jared had always liked his living space to be simple and uncluttered.

Apart from some green plants, the only splashes of colour were provided by pictures, one of which, with its kaleidoscope of colour-washed houses spilling down the hillside to the blue, blue sea, she recognized as the Italian town of Portofino.

Jared had promised that one day it would be their honeymoon destination.

Gazing at it, she swallowed and, her throat feeling as though it were full of shards of hot glass, wondered if he had taken his wife there.

Only as she started to turn away did she realize that his eyes were on her face, noting her reaction.

'A lovely spot,' he remarked. 'I've always thought it an ideal place for a honeymoon.'

Touched on the raw, she said dismissively, 'In Martin's opinion, Italy's old hat these days. He's planning to take me to Dubai for our honeymoon.'

She hadn't wanted to go to Dubai, considering it soulless and unromantic. But, feeling the need to please Martin, she had said nothing.

Jared's white teeth flashed in the semblance of a smile. 'Well, bully for him.'

Something about that wolfish grin made Perdita wish fervently that she had kept her mouth shut.

But, a moment later, his face impassive, he pointed to an archway on the right. 'The main living quarters are that way, while the bedrooms are at this end of the house.'

He led her through another white archway and down a wide corridor to a door about two-thirds along. 'This is my room,' he told her.

As he paused to put his case inside, she caught a glimpse of a king-sized bed and a colour scheme of off-white and mint-green that looked cool and fresh.

Moving to the next door along, he said casually, 'And this is yours.'

A matching white-painted tongue-and-groove door opened into another large, attractive bedroom with an off-white carpet and pale lilac walls.

Between the two rooms was a communicating door, and a glass door with an ornate white metal grille led on to the veranda.

Seeing her eyes were fixed on the communicating door, Jared said ironically, 'It isn't locked, and we don't seem to have a key. But if it'll make you any happier, feel free to put a chair under the handle.'

Ignoring the taunt, she glanced around. There was the minimum of light modern furniture, but the bed was king-sized and, with its lightweight white and mauve duvet, looked comfortable and inviting.

Both the windows were open and the muslin curtains moved idly in the gentle breeze.

Putting her case on a low chest, Jared said, 'When you've unpacked and freshened up, we'll have a spot of supper.'

'I'd prefer to go straight to bed,' she told him and braced herself for an argument.

'What about a cup of tea or coffee? Or a cool drink, perhaps?'

She shook her head silently.

Watching her and noting the stubborn set of her jaw, he sighed inwardly. Of course he *could* beat down any opposition, but for the moment he would much prefer to use the softly-softly approach.

With that in mind, his tone eminently reasonable, he said, 'The only problem is, if you do go straight to bed, you may find yourself lying wide awake in the early hours of the morning.

'The best means of beating the time difference is to stay awake until it's bedtime here. That way, your body clock adjusts much faster… But of course it's entirely up to you. If you do decide to join me, I'll be on the terrace at the far end of the house.'

Perdita had expected opposition and she breathed a sigh of relief that he had been so reasonable. Perhaps things wouldn't be quite as bad as she had anticipated, although it was early days yet.

Reluctant as she was, knowing it wouldn't help matters to have creased clothes, she began to unpack her case.

Sally had put in light, easy-to-wear mix and match things, some pretty undies and nightwear, a good selection of accessories and even the blue velvet box that held her small amount of jewellery.

She had, Perdita was forced to admit, chosen well and packed with care.

When she had put her ivory satin nightdress and negligée on the bed, she stowed the rest of her things in the large walk-in wardrobe. Then, taking her toilet bag through to the en suite bathroom, she tucked her hair beneath a shower cap and enjoyed a warm shower.

Having dried herself on soft fluffy towels, she brushed her hair into a silken mass and plaited it loosely into a single thick braid, before brushing her teeth ready for the night.

Back in her bedroom, she put on her nightdress and went to look out of the window. The scented air was warm and clear as glass, the view green and pleasant. In the wooded area beyond the garden, she could hear the murmur of a stream and the endless shrilling of the cicadas.

The sun had slipped below the horizon in a blaze of glory, while the rest of the sky, though still clear and blue, had lost its earlier brightness and was waiting for evening.

Perdita had always thought there was something a little sad, a little melancholy, about this time of the day. But now she felt a much deeper sadness, a kind of forlorn isolation that made her heart as heavy as lead and weighed down her spirits.

Sighing, she tried to tell herself that she was missing Martin, missing his reassuring presence. But in reality, since being with Jared, she had hardly given Martin a thought.

What *was* weighing down her spirits was the knowledge that Jared was married. She knew quite well that it shouldn't matter a jot to her, that she should be pleased. But somehow, in spite of everything, it *did* matter, and she was anything but pleased.

Don't be a fool, she chided herself. She had had her chance and, unable to trust him, had chosen to have her freedom.

And now she was going to marry Martin—she touched the sparkling engagement ring on her finger as if it were a talisman—Martin, who was trustworthy and reliable, who adored her and wrapped her in a warm, comforting blanket of security.

Martin, who had never managed to quicken her breathing or raise her pulse rate one iota.

What was she doing marrying a man she didn't love and would never love in the way a woman should love her husband?

The sudden honesty was searing and, stripped of all pretence, she felt shaken and very much alone.

Normally she had no problem being on her own, and quite often preferred it that way. But now she found herself fidgety and restless.

She didn't even have a book with her, so the only sensible thing she could do was go to bed. But, remembering Jared's warning, she hesitated.

The last thing she wanted was to find herself lying awake

in the early hours of the morning, uneasy thoughts churning round and round in her brain.

There was one other option, she admitted. An option she had been trying to push to the back of her mind. Now, however, it came to the fore and steadfastly refused to be banished.

She could go and join Jared.

Such a move might prove to be a bad mistake, she warned herself. On the other hand, this could be her last chance to see him, to be with him, before his wife arrived.

Galvanized by that thought, she took off her nightdress and, unconsciously hurrying, pulled on fresh undies, a pair of oatmeal trousers and a loose silky top in burnt chocolate.

Then, leaving her face shiny and her hair in its thick, loose braid, she plucked up her courage and ventured forth.

CHAPTER FIVE

EVERYWHERE was silent and there was no sign of the house-keeper, but presumably she would have her own quarters, Perdita thought as she made her way through the hall to the far end of the house.

Opening the door into an attractive and spacious living room, she found it was sparsely but beautifully furnished with well chosen antiques.

There was an off-white carpet and, standing in front of a huge fireplace of unplastered stone, a cushioned couch and two armchairs upholstered in coffee-coloured linen.

Either side of the fireplace there were tall eighteenth century bookcases, complete with a graceful pulpit staircase.

On the chimney breast hung a modern oil painting, a striking Tuscan scene by Marco Abruzzi. In the background were fields of vivid yellow sunflowers, vibrant with colour and warmth, and closer at hand a group of farm buildings, sunbaked and tumbledown, that were patterned with blue-black shadows.

Such a juxtaposition of old and new shouldn't have worked. But, against all the odds, it did.

The room itself was high and open to the rafters and painted the palest of greens, which made it feel cool and airy, while the end wall was almost entirely made up of sliding glass panels.

Through the glass, Perdita caught sight of Jared sitting in a lounger on the paved terrace, a tall glass in his hand.

All at once she knew her decision to come had been a mistake. Instead of letting herself be drawn to his side, she should have stayed safely in her room.

She was about to turn and hurry back when, as though sensing her presence, he glanced up and, rising to his feet, loose-limbed and relaxed, smiled at her.

Perdita had the strangest feeling that he had been expecting her, that he had *willed* her to come.

He reached to press a button and, as the glass panels slid aside, invited, 'Do come and join us for a drink.'

Us.

Her heart plummeted. Did that mean his wife had already arrived?

Apparently it did, for, as she stood frozen, he urged, 'Sam and I would be honoured if you'd grace us with your company.'

So his wife's name was Samantha…

But while the thought was still going through Perdita's mind, as if the use of his name had disturbed him, the biggest dog she had ever seen came bounding in from the terrace. Putting his paws on her shoulders, making her stagger back, he laved her face with a warm pink tongue.

Laughing, the tension momentarily broken, she made a valiant effort to push him down, but he was as heavy as he was affectionate and it took a firm command from Jared to stop the friendly assault.

Stroking his massive head, she said, an edge of relief in her voice, 'Well, hello, Sam. So where did you spring from?'

'He lives here,' Jared told her, 'though he stays with Hilary while I'm not at home.

'She thinks he's cute,' he added, tongue in cheek. 'Though he's only a pup and still learning, she told me that Sam's the smartest dog she's ever known.'

Perdita was still smiling at the thought of the huge dog being described as *cute* when he turned and offered her an outsized paw.

Smiling, Jared said, 'He's taken quite a fancy to you, haven't you, Sam?'

Addressing the dog, Perdita asked in mock reproof, 'If it's true that you're so smart, why don't you speak for yourself?'

With a sigh, Jared said, 'I don't know how to break this to you, but he's a little shy.'

She gave a choke of laughter as, his thick tail whacking against her legs, Sam escorted her out onto the terrace before flopping down again by his master's chair.

Having settled her into one of the cushioned loungers, Jared studied her shiny face and bedtime braid with interest.

Feeling the colour rise in her cheeks, and wishing she had stopped to do her hair and put on a touch of make-up, she said in confusion, 'I must look an absolute fright.'

'Not that I've noticed.'

As she put up her hands to undo the braid, he caught them and stopped her. 'Leave it. It's quite charming.' And indeed he thought he'd never seen a lovelier picture than she made at that moment.

He released her hands and, subduing a powerful urge to bend his head and kiss her pale lips, enquired prosaically, 'What would you like to drink?'

Shaken by his touch, she managed, 'Something long and cool, please.'

Over to one side was a small semi-circular bar complete with a fridge and a coffee-making machine and, beyond that, a drinking fountain and a comprehensive barbecue and grill.

Watching him cross to the bar, she noticed that he had changed into pale cream trousers and a dark green sports shirt, short-sleeved and open at the neck to expose his tanned throat.

In spite of all the travelling they had done that day, he looked fresh and coolly elegant, and disturbingly attractive.

Taking a squat glass pitcher from the fridge, chinking with ice, he filled a tall frosted tumbler and, handing it to her, said, 'Try that and see what you think.'

She took a sip of the fruity concoction. 'Mmm...that's delicious.'

'Good.'

Taking his seat, he stretched his long legs indolently, while they sat in what might almost have passed for a companionable silence if there hadn't been an edge of tension.

Tension which she recognized as her own.

In an effort to beat it, she gestured towards the open glass panels and, like a polite guest, remarked, 'You have a really lovely room.'

He smiled a little mockingly but, donning the mantle of an equally polite host, he answered, 'I'm so glad you like it.'

Gritting her teeth, she battled on. 'I was a bit surprised to find a fireplace.'

'Well, as you know, the Californian weather isn't *always* good and sometimes, especially in the cooler evenings, I enjoy the cosiness, the *intimacy*, of a nice log fire. If I remember rightly, you used to enjoy it too.'

A sudden memory took her by the throat. A memory of them stretched out in front of a blazing log fire while he ran skilful hands over her naked body.

She recalled the feel of those long sensitive fingers caressing her breasts, teasing the pink nipples, stroking down her flat stomach to twine themselves in the tangle of pale golden curls...

Her breath coming fast, she strove to banish the erotic pictures from her mind, but the damage was already done.

And he knew, of course.

Trying to douse the heat that engulfed her from head to toe, she took a too hasty gulp of her drink and choked.

'Dear me,' Jared said mildly as he removed the glass from her unsteady fingers while she coughed, 'I didn't think I'd put that much alcohol in it. Or was it something I said?'

When she regained her voice, she told him huskily, 'I just swallowed down the wrong way.'

'You'll have to be more careful. It's made you go quite pink.'

Biting her lip, she accepted her glass back and, desperate to regain at least an outward appearance of coolness, looked around.

A wing of the house ran at right angles to the roofed terrace, so that it was enclosed on two sides. The remaining two, which could be screened off with sliding glass panels, looked along the valley and across to the steeply wooded slope that rose way beyond the gardens.

At the other end of the terrace, a creeper-clad garage block flanked a wide green lawn which appeared to run down to a sunken garden. In the middle of the lawn was a magnificent cedar tree with a hammock slung from its sturdy boughs.

Closer at hand, just beyond the paved patio area, a large swimming pool looked blue and inviting and mirror-calm.

To one side of the pool was an open-air jacuzzi, a couple of white-painted changing cabins and what she took to be a sauna. Beyond those was a wooden building with long windows that appeared to house a small gym.

It seemed that Wolf Rock lacked for nothing.

But by now, she reminded herself, the man her father had said contemptuously would never have amounted to anything must be a multi-millionaire.

Though she held out very little hope that in the end Jared would save JB Electronics, in spite of everything, she found herself oddly pleased that her father had been wrong.

Thinking of all the company's financial problems and what they had led to, particularly in her case, she shivered.

Proving that he never missed a thing, Jared raised an eyebrow and queried, 'Cold?'

'No. No... It's lovely out here. It was just someone walking over my grave.'

Jared got up to replenish their glasses and, as he resumed his seat, his voice studiedly casual, he asked, 'What do you think of Wolf Rock so far?'

'I think it's beautiful,' she answered.

He looked pleased. 'Tomorrow I'll show you over the winery itself, if you're interested.'

'Oh, yes,' she said, eagerness in her voice. 'Seeing how the wine's made should be quite fascinating.'

Then, happy that it was a nice safe topic of conversation, she pursued, 'Do you know why it's called Wolf Rock?'

He pointed over what appeared to be extensive gardens. 'See where the ground begins to rise steeply, there's a break in the trees about halfway up the slope...'

'Yes.'

'If you can see well enough in this light, there's a large rock jutting out that looks remarkably like the head of a wolf in profile...'

'Yes, yes, I see it,' she said.

Perhaps it was the touch of excitement in her voice that made Sam get up, thrust his huge head into her lap and gaze up at her adoringly.

'Why, you're just a big softy,' she told him.

Clearly wanting more than mere words, he nudged her hand with a big black nose.

She responded by stroking him, and laughed as he snuffled rapturously.

'Fancy you wanting all this fuss.'

'He's jealous,' Jared told her. 'Has been ever since he realized he was being upstaged by a wolf. However, we can easily divert him.'

'How?'

'Simply by mentioning the word *food*…'

The dog immediately lifted his head and sat to attention, looking at his master.

'He's still got a puppy's appetite,' Jared explained, 'so he's always ready to eat… Speaking of which, are you happy to eat out here?'

'Quite happy, if it won't bother your housekeeper.'

'Hilary organizes everything. When she knows I'm coming, she leaves a meal ready and then goes home to her husband.'

'Oh…'

Seeing the sudden unease she wasn't able to hide, a glint in his eye, he said, 'I hope it doesn't bother you that we're here alone?'

'No, why should it?' Knowing she'd sounded anything but convincing, she added, 'After all, you're a married man.'

'I am indeed,' he agreed with some satisfaction.

All her previous melancholy closing in once more, she realized unhappily that coming to join him had solved nothing, and she tried to think of a good excuse to get out of eating with him.

She still hadn't found one when, indicating the wing that ran alongside the terrace, he suggested quizzically, 'As you and Sam have been…shall we say…up close and personal, there's a cloakroom through there if you'd like to rinse off before we have supper.'

Putting her empty glass on the low table between the loungers, she got to her feet and began, 'On second thoughts, I'm not really hungry. If you don't mind, I'll skip supper and go straight back to—'

Rising with her, he broke in firmly, 'But I *do* mind. As you may remember, I've never much cared for eating alone.'

He took her chin, fingers spread on one side, thumb on

the other, and tilted her face up to his, making the protest die on her lips.

'I want you to stay.'

Silvery eyes met and held blue-green and, as with Guinevere and Lancelot, hers fell first.

'Very well,' she mumbled.

As soon as he released her she turned and, trembling in every limb, fled to the well equipped cloakroom to wash her face and hands.

When she reluctantly returned, she found Sam had been banished to the far side of the terrace with a lion-sized bowl of food which he was golloping with noisy enjoyment.

To Perdita's surprise, the table had been set with linen napkins, crystal glasses and a tall red candle in an onyx holder.

On a side trolley there was a platter of cheeses and a bowl of fruit and, on a hotplate, several dishes were keeping warm.

Watching her expressive face, Jared grinned and queried, 'Impressed?'

'Very. I confess I'd expected something a great deal more casual.'

Having pulled out a chair for her, he explained, 'Where quite a lot of the local people tend to eat casually when it's alfresco, Hilary believes that good food should be served in style.'

A purple dusk was falling now, and he lit the candle before settling Perdita at the table and helping them both to a glass of chilled white wine and a bowl of lobster bisque.

Raising his glass, he suggested, 'Shall we drink to a successful outcome to our negotiations?'

'Successful for whom?' she asked a shade tartly.

He laughed and saluted her spirit, before querying, 'Isn't true success achieved only when both parties get what they want?'

After a moment, she admitted a shade helplessly, 'I still don't know for sure what you *do* want.'

When he just looked at her without speaking, she said

vexedly, 'I think it's high time you told me why you went to so much trouble to get me out here.'

'I suggest that we eat first and talk later,' he said, his voice even. 'It would be a shame if the soup got cold.'

Seeing nothing else for it, Perdita bit back her impatience and applied herself to the bisque, which proved to be excellent.

It was followed by baked trout with almonds, and artichoke hearts with a beurre blanc sauce.

When her plate was empty, Perdita sighed and admitted, 'Your housekeeper is a wonderful cook.'

'I'll tell her you said so; she's always pleased when people enjoy her meals. She firmly believes, as I do, that good food is one of life's pleasures. Now, try a little of this cheese...'

When they had finished the cheese course he filled their coffee cups and, producing a fine old brandy, poured them each a generous measure.

Perdita, who normally drank very little, had already enjoyed two glasses of wine and was starting to feel a little light-headed. But, trying a cautious sip, she found it tasted smooth and mellow and relatively innocent.

Even so, she decided, it might be wise to drink her coffee first.

As she picked up her cup, Sam came ambling over and, settling himself in front of her, he sat up and begged clumsily, waving his front paws as if trying to keep his balance.

'Oh, look at him!' she exclaimed, laughing. Then, to the dog, 'You really are a smart pup, but I'm afraid I don't know what you want.'

'He wants some coffee,' Jared told her.

'Surely you don't give him coffee?'

'No, not as a rule, but Hilary does.'

Reaching over, Jared covered the dog's big ears before whispering, 'She's trying to stunt his growth. Though I'm inclined to think she may have left it a little too late.'

Perdita gave a gurgle of laughter. 'A lot too late, if you ask me.'

'Oh, well, I suppose I'd better pour him some,' Jared said good-naturedly and rose to his feet. 'Otherwise we'll get no peace.'

When the dog had been provided with a bowl of milky coffee, Jared resumed his seat and sipped his own coffee in silence.

He seemed to have lapsed into a reflective mood. But, thinking back to her earlier question and determined to get an answer this time, Perdita took a deep breath and said, 'Now we've finished our meal, perhaps you'll be kind enough to tell me exactly why you brought me here. There has to be a reason.'

A little smile twisting his chiselled lips, he said, 'I thought you'd made up your mind that it was just to exact revenge?'

'I can't see what else it could possibly be.'

'If I may say so, that shows a remarkable lack of imagination on your part.' The merest hint of a threat in his tone, he added, 'There are other equally interesting reasons.'

In an attempt to hide the sudden quiver that ran through her, she said challengingly, 'Perhaps you'd like to tell me what they are?'

'Firstly, I thought it might be time to give things a second chance.'

'What do you mean by that?'

'Exactly what I say.'

Seeing he had no intention of elaborating, she bit her lip before returning to the attack. 'But "giving things a second chance" isn't the only reason?'

'No.' Candlelight gleamed in his eyes, turning the silver to gold. 'There was a far more pressing one.'

'And what was that?' she asked, trying hard to hide her apprehension.

She was both surprised and shocked when he said flatly, 'I couldn't allow you to go ahead and marry Judson.'

'*Allow* me to marry Martin!' she choked. 'There's no way you can stop me.'

'I wouldn't be too sure about that…' He rose to his feet with an easy masculine grace. 'Shall we have some more coffee?'

Why was he so set against her marrying Martin? she wondered as she watched him fill the coffee cups.

But, whatever his reasons, she told herself stoutly, there was no way he could prevent the marriage. He couldn't keep her in the States indefinitely.

Perhaps his plan was to make *not* marrying Martin part of a deal to save JB Electronics?

If it was, where would that leave her?

Though she felt dreadfully disloyal, honesty made her admit that she couldn't claim she would be heartbroken. But if she *was* forced to cancel the wedding, Martin was bound to be badly hurt.

No, she couldn't—wouldn't—do that to him. He didn't deserve it.

Returning with the coffee, Jared suggested, 'Suppose we move back to the loungers to drink it?'

When they were both settled in the loungers, as though he'd been given a signal, Sam came over and settled himself at his master's side.

While Jared absently fondled the hound's ears, determined to have some answers, Perdita asked, 'Why don't you want me to marry Martin?'

As he looked at her levelly, she hurried on, 'I know there's no love lost between the pair of you, but surely it has to be more than that?'

'You're quite right. In fact, I have two very good reasons. Firstly, I don't believe you love him—'

'I do,' she insisted. 'Passionately. But what can it possibly matter to you whether or not I love him?'

'It matters quite a lot.'

About to challenge him on that, she chickened out and instead asked, 'And what's the second reason?'

'He's not good enough for you.'

Feeling the need to defend Martin, she cried, 'Let me tell you that as well as being loyal and faithful, he's one of the nicest, kindest men I've ever met. He's straightforward and honest. He hasn't a nasty bone in his body.'

Jared's white teeth flashed in a mirthless smile. 'I'm afraid you're deluding yourself. He's cunning and deceitful, and a liar to boot.'

'How can you make such accusations?' she stormed. 'They're just not true.'

'They're true enough.'

'I don't know what makes you think that. Martin's incapable of lies and deceit.'

His voice full of bitterness, Jared said, 'If only you'd championed *me* like that.'

'I would have done if you'd been worth it,' she flashed, and saw his face turn pale, as if the words were rocks she'd hit him with.

Suddenly she would have given a lot to have left them unspoken, and she felt the quick prick of tears behind her eyes.

When she had succeeded in getting her emotions under control, she made an effort to battle on. 'Let's suppose I agreed to call the wedding off... Is that all you want?'

A razor-sharp edge to his voice, he said, 'Not by a long chalk.'

There was, she saw, a complete change in his manner. Before she'd spoken those fatal words, though always the man in command, he had appeared relatively relaxed and easy.

True he had been a tough, challenging opponent, but an attractive, charismatic one.

Now he was wholly formidable and frightening, a man who would have no mercy and give no quarter.

All his previous hardness was back, and it showed in the

tightness of his jaw, the ruthless set of his lips, and the silvery-grey eyes that were as cold and bleak as any glacier.

She shivered. But if she let him see she was afraid, she would be lost.

That thought in mind, she said with far more boldness than she felt, 'I think it's about time you stopped playing games with me and told me in words of one syllable just what it is you *do* want.'

'In words of one syllable, I want *you*.'

She sat mute and frozen, trying to tell herself she had misheard but knowing she hadn't.

'It seems to have come as a shock to you,' he observed sardonically.

Somehow she found her voice. 'But you told me you were married.'

'I *am* married.'

Stammering a little, she said, 'Then I…I don't…I just don't understand.'

'Is *I want you* so very difficult to understand?'

'In spite of the fact that you have a wife, you're asking me to share your bed?'

His dark, handsome face looking cold and implacable, he told her, 'I'm not *asking* you anything. I'm *telling* you.'

'You must be joking,' she said shakily. 'What would your wife say if she…'

Something about his expression alerted her, and the words faltered and died on her lips as, belatedly, realization began to dawn.

The last remnants of colour draining from her face, she stared at him in startled silence.

'I can see you're finally getting there,' he said with grim satisfaction.

Unwilling to believe it, she whispered, 'You can't mean that I'm…?'

'Still my wife? That's exactly what I mean.'

Through stiff lips she accused, 'You didn't have our marriage annulled, after all!'

'No, I didn't…' he said evenly.

It had been a whirlwind affair in a small chapel just outside Las Vegas, a marriage that was no marriage, that had never been consummated.

'And, while our wedding wasn't particularly romantic,' he went on flatly, 'it was legal and binding. We're still man and wife…'

So that was why he couldn't let her marry Martin.

As though reading her mind, Jared reached for her hand and, slipping off her engagement ring, dropped it into his shirt pocket. 'Which means it's high time we got rid of this.'

Still struggling to take in what he'd told her, she failed to protest.

In truth, the huge diamond solitaire on its platinum band had never meant half as much to her as the gold ring Jared had given her, with its pale turquoise stone that, he had told her, matched her beautiful eyes.

But that had been a long time ago, and so much had happened since then to spoil a love she had once considered perfect.

Finding they were still married had been a shock, scattering her wits like a shotgun blast scattered starlings and jarring her mind so that it seemed incapable of functioning.

After a moment, from amongst the welter of confusion, one thing that had been niggling at her, painful as a sore tooth, suddenly surfaced.

Lifting her head, she said slowly, 'You told Sally we were still married. That's the reason she agreed to help you.'

'It was one of the reasons.'

Though the last thing Perdita had wanted or expected was to find herself still tied to Jared, it was a relief to be able to acquit a woman she had grown to like and respect.

After a moment, she gathered herself and said, 'I don't understand *why* you didn't have the marriage annulled. It had never been consummated, and I sent you all the necessary papers and sworn affidavits.'

'I didn't want an annulment,' he said evenly. 'I wanted my wife back.'

Her normally low, slightly husky voice sounding high and shrill even in her own ears, she cried, 'Now I understand. But if you think for one instant that I'd be willing to come back to you, you're crazy.'

'If I am,' he said grimly, 'it's because you've made me that way. But, crazy or not, they are my terms. If you want to save your father any further worry and stress and keep his company afloat, you'll need to agree to them.'

'Well, if this is your idea of *negotiating*, you've been wasting your time. I've absolutely no intention of agreeing to them.'

'As always, it's up to you,' he said evenly. 'But there's quite a lot at stake, so you might want to think about it before you refuse.'

He was right about there being a lot at stake, but she couldn't sink her pride and go back to him, she just *couldn't*!

He stayed silent, giving her time, and after a minute or so she asked, as he had surely known she would, 'And presumably you would still want a controlling interest in the company?'

He shook his head. 'I'll settle for fifty per cent of the shares.'

'So what exactly are you offering in return for me and fifty per cent of the shares?' Her voice shook, making her attempt at sarcasm a miserable failure.

His manner businesslike and to the point, he said, 'As soon as I have your agreement, I'll buy the shares at the full market price and pay off the mortgage on your father's house as well as all the bank loans and overdrafts.

'I'll also provide an immediate injection of cash.' He named a sum that made her blink. 'And if I judge that the new projects you mentioned are worth it, I'll provide ample funds to finance them through to completion.'

Trying to take it in and feeling a little dazed, she asked, 'Would you mind saying all that again?'

He repeated word for word what he had just said.

It was a much more generous offer than she might have dared to expect or hope for, and the consequences of refusing would be dire.

The company her father and Elmer had spent a lifetime building up would go down the drain. Their loyal employees would lose their jobs and, instead of her father and Elmer being able to retire comfortably, they would end up bankrupt and without a roof over their heads.

Common sense told her that Martin and Elmer would be able to weather the storm somehow, but in her father's case it was bound to put a serious strain on his heart.

Yet how could she bring herself to live with a man she no longer loved? A man she was more than half afraid of? A man from whose dark spell she had struggled so hard to escape…?

While turbulent thoughts tumbled through her mind, she stared blindly at the hands clasped tightly together in her lap, desperately seeking a solution when common sense told her there wasn't one.

His eyes fixed on her down-bent face, Jared finally broke the silence to ask, 'Well? Have you decided?'

Lifting her head, she took a deep shuddering breath and, trying to sound firm but only managing to sound panic-stricken and desperate, said, 'I can't give you an answer straight away. I need time to think about it.'

'Very well. I'll give you twenty-four hours.'

Twenty-four hours wasn't long, but it was at least a breathing space, a temporary reprieve from having to make such a traumatic decision.

CHAPTER SIX

WHILE PERDITA had been caught up in a maelstrom of turbulent thoughts, the last traces of evening had flown and a starlit night had taken its place.

Though the air was still soft and balmy, a faint breeze had sprung up and was stirring the tendrils of the flowering vine that hung close by, sending its perfume drifting seductively.

She recalled such a lovely night years ago in San Jose. A perfect starlit, romantic night when, having told her father she was sleeping over with a friend, she had slipped away from the party early and gone to Jared's house.

After they had eaten supper on his patio, he had surprised her by slipping a ring onto her finger and asking her formally to marry him.

Her heart overflowing, she had accepted, with the proviso that they kept their engagement a secret for the time being at least.

Until then, because of her father's opposition, their relationship, though passionate, had been confined to kisses and caresses, and talk of "being together" once her father was well enough.

Since their first meeting, Jared had treated her as the innocent she was, but that night, as they sat together on the swing seat, eager to be his in every sense of the word, *she* had made the running.

After undoing his shirt buttons, she had slid her hands inside, running them over his muscular chest, finding the sprinkling of crisp body hair and the small leathery nipples.

When she'd felt him get restive beneath her touch, she'd started to unfasten the clip on the waistband of his trousers. Catching hold of her hands, he had held them away and asked with mock severity, 'I hope you know what you're doing?'

'I'm turning you on,' she had answered daringly. 'Or, rather, I'm trying to.'

'You're succeeding,' he had warned her grimly. 'So, unless you're prepared to take the consequences...'

'Yes, please,' she had whispered, lifting her face for his kiss, and hand in hand they had walked into the house.

It had been the most wonderful night of her life, a night that had seen her transformed from a naive girl into a woman.

Though a complete innocent, she had tendered passion for passion with a joyous abandon that had filled Jared's heart with gladness.

Afterwards, lying in his arms, his ring on her finger, her happiness and contentment had been complete. He had proved to be a marvellous lover, not only masterful and heartbreakingly tender, but skilled and experienced.

That last thought had brought a slight cloud of unease and jealousy with it. Though he was the right type to be a good lover—generous, unselfish and passionate—she was well aware that all his skill and experience had needed to be *acquired*.

Biting her lip, she had tried hard to push that sudden doubt to the back of her mind.

The following morning before she went home, he had bought her an antique gold chain with a chunky gold locket that opened to hold the ring. Fastening it round her neck, he had said, 'Now you can wear it next to your heart until we can tell the world.'

He had added that he would always love her and promised to be faithful, and she had believed him.

More fool her.

All the old bitterness and disillusionment returned in full force, reminding her, if such a reminder was necessary, just why she couldn't face the thought of going back to him.

A fresh rush of agitation brought her to her feet. 'If you don't mind, I'd like to go to bed now,' she said jerkily.

Though he frowned a little, as if he'd been following her train of thought, he agreed levelly, 'It's been a long day so I think I'll join you.'

She stiffened. Suppose he meant that literally?

But he had turned away and was snapping his fingers at the dog. 'Come on, Sam. Bed time.'

They made their way into the house and Jared closed and locked the glass panels before shutting Sam in the kitchen.

Unable to judge from Jared's expression exactly what his intentions were, Perdita held her breath as he escorted her along to her bedroom.

Having opened the door for her, he made no attempt to follow her inside but simply said, 'Goodnight, Perdita. Sleep well.'

'Goodnight,' she answered huskily.

She was about to turn away when he lifted her chin and kissed her lightly on the lips. Though he wasn't holding her in any way, that sweetest of caresses kept her rooted to the spot.

Even when he lifted his head and walked away, she stayed exactly where she was, still as any statue, until the sound of his bedroom door closing brought her back to life.

Forcing her weak knees to carry her into her own room, she shut the door behind her and slumped limply against it.

If he'd taken her in his arms, deepened the kiss...

But he hadn't.

She felt a quick surge of what she tried to tell herself was relief.

But mingled with that relief was a tingle of something she recognized as regret, and she was forced to admit that at some fundamental level she still wanted him.

No! she corrected herself quickly, she *couldn't* still want him after all that had happened. That strong physical attraction must simply be because she had suppressed her basic needs for so long that her body was starting to rebel.

But, if that was the case, why had she kept Martin, a man who thought the world of her, at arm's length?

She sighed and, in an endeavour to stop herself thinking, went through to the pleasant bathroom and prepared for bed once more.

When she had slipped beneath the light duvet, she closed her eyes and made an effort to empty her mind, but sleep steadfastly eluded her.

Trapped once more on the endless treadmill of thought, it was the early hours of the morning before her weary brain stopped working and she finally fell into an uneasy doze.

She awoke to a strange room filled with sunlight. For a moment or two her mind was a complete blank, and then everything that had happened the previous evening came back in a rush.

She was still Jared's wife. Nominally. And in a matter of hours she would have to decide whether or not to go back to him.

Every nerve in her body tightened and a rising panic threatened to engulf her. Forcing it down, she climbed out of bed and pulled back the light muslin curtains. The sun was riding high in the sky, and a glance at her watch showed it was almost midday.

When she had showered and dressed in a blue and white striped shirtwaister and sandals, she brushed out her long hair and pulled it back into a loose gleaming knot.

It had been her intention to leave by way of the veranda,

but the glass door refused to open and the lock was empty, so she made her way through the silent house.

There was no sign of the housekeeper, but the complete absence of dust and the bowls of fresh flowers suggested that that good lady had been busy.

On the opposite side of the hallway a door leading on to the far veranda was standing invitingly open, and crossing to it, Perdita stepped out into the fresh air.

From here she got a panoramic view over a wide swathe of picturesque countryside. In the distance, lush and green, she could see row upon row of vines while a crop-spraying helicopter, with a trail of fine spray suspended beneath it like a cloud, clattered noisily up the valley.

As she walked along the veranda looking at the adobe walls and the tubs of bright flowers, mingling with the sweet scent of the flowers she became aware of an appetizing smell of grilled bacon and percolating coffee.

When she reached the south side of the house and the pool area, she descended the veranda steps into the blazing sun. The house and the veranda had been relatively cool and only then, standing looking around her, did she appreciate just how hot it was.

She had always enjoyed the heat and, after a long cold winter in London, it was very welcome.

All traces of the previous evening had been cleared away and by the pool a white table, shielded from the full strength of the sun by a canopy of vines, had been set for brunch.

On the side trolley was a tall glass jug of orange juice, a basket of newly baked rolls, a tub of butter and a selection of preserves, while several covered dishes and a pot of coffee were keeping warm on the hotplate.

Sam ambled over to greet her, languid in the heat, and offered her a huge clumsy paw before returning to his post by the table, where an empty bowl waited to be filled.

Jared was in the water, doing lengths in a fast effortless crawl. He was in the middle of a racing turn at the far end of the pool when he saw her.

Levering himself out in one smooth movement, he shook the water out of his eyes and walked towards her, his smile a challenge.

He was stark naked and very male.

A betraying heat ran through her and her stomach clenched as, unable to tear her gaze away, she watched him approach.

The sun gleamed on his smooth skin and rivulets of water ran down his muscular body. With broad shoulders, lean hips and long supple limbs, he had a classical beauty that—though the concept was hackneyed—she had always thought of as godlike.

Every inch of his skin appeared to be deeply tanned and, with the dark hair curling on his chest and the gleam of his white teeth as he smiled at her, he could almost have been Greek.

'Good morning. Sleep well?'

Forcing herself to take a breath, she lied, 'Very well, thank you.' Then, looking anywhere but at him, 'Brunch by the pool, I see.'

'Naturally. You're in sunny California now.' He surveyed her dress critically. 'Though, to enjoy it to the full, you could do with rather fewer clothes.'

Her eyes skittering nervously past his nakedness, she hoped he didn't mean what she thought he meant.

Reading her unease and interpreting it correctly, he laughed and added, 'A bikini, for example.'

'I haven't owned a bikini, or a swimsuit of any kind, since I left California,' she told him.

'Well, after we've had brunch we can easily remedy that, and a little sunshine is all you need to banish that winter paleness.'

It was an enticing thought. But the last thing she wanted to do was wear any kind of swimsuit in front of Jared.

Though she loved the sun, she had always been inhibited

about baring her body, and it was he who had first encouraged her to strip off and enjoy the feel of the sun on her bare skin.

And she was lucky. Unlike the pale, ultra-sensitive skin of a lot of natural blondes, her skin tanned well and easily to a pale burnished gold.

Picking up a towel from one of the poolside sunbeds, Jared knotted it casually around his lean waist before leading the way to the table, leaving wet footprints on the decking.

He settled her in one of the white chairs before taking a seat opposite and asking cheerfully, 'Juice to start with?'

'Please.'

Sitting in the dappled shade, she sipped the freshly squeezed juice and, finding it deliciously cool and sweet, murmured, 'Mmm... I don't know why, but that tastes so much nicer than we get in London.'

With a quick grin, he suggested, 'Perhaps it's because, unlike California, they don't grow oranges in London.'

Smiling back spontaneously, she agreed, 'You could be right.'

Watching that smile light her face and bring it to life, Jared observed a shade huskily, 'You should smile more often. It suits you.'

Flicked on the raw, she retorted, 'I haven't had a lot to smile about just recently.'

Instantly regretting her own sharpness, she was pleased when he seemed disposed to ignore it.

When their glasses were empty, he helped her to crisp bacon, scrambled eggs and waffles, before pouring the fragrant coffee.

Seeing the play of muscles beneath his smooth tanned skin, she felt her heartbeat quicken. With his hair still wet and rumpled, his broad shoulders and chest and the strong column of his throat bare, he looked so disturbingly sexy that she was finding it difficult to breathe, let alone eat.

But it was more than just his looks. It always had been.

Watching his face, a face she knew as well as she knew her own, she remembered how it was when they had first met and got to know each other.

For her, they had been weeks of discovery, of delight. Slowly, she had learnt that he was never dull, never disappointing, never mean or small-minded, never at a loss.

They had been in perfect harmony. He seemed able to read her mind and know what she was thinking, and if he wasn't with her he was one step ahead, waiting for her to catch up.

But, best of all, she'd discovered she could be herself with him. Neither her shyness nor her inhibitions, her occasional short bursts of temper or the fact that at times—having been overindulged and pampered all her life—she was unwittingly selfish, bothered him. He accepted her faults as gracefully as he welcomed her merits.

Knowing him had freed her from the suffocating restrictions of her childhood, and turned her into a well balanced adult, able to think for herself.

Well balanced? Able to think for herself? Was that really a true picture?

The last three years seemed to suggest it wasn't. She was still following her father's lead, still allowing him to influence and mollycoddle her.

And if she *had* married Martin, as her father's chosen ambassador, *he* would have carried on where the older man had left off...

Suddenly becoming aware that Jared had said something she hadn't caught, Perdita glanced up in confusion. 'I'm sorry?'

'I said, if we're to buy that bikini I'd better get showered and dressed.'

'I don't need a bikini, really I don't.'

'You prefer to swim and sunbathe in the nude?'

Grinning at her horrified expression, he said briskly, 'So

you need a bikini, or at least a costume of some kind. Give me ten minutes and we'll have a trip into Napa.'

Hoping to deflect him from his purpose, she protested, 'But you promised you'd take me round the winery, and I'd much rather do that.'

Not taken in for a moment, he said lightly, 'Don't worry, we can do both.'

When he returned, well within the promised time, looking casually elegant in well-cut lightweight trousers and a midnight-blue silk shirt, he was carrying a high factor sunscreen and a spare pair of sunglasses.

She glimpsed the old ever-thoughtful Jared when, handing them to her, he said, 'You're not yet used to this kind of sun, so you may need both of these.'

Grateful for his consideration, she said a sincere, 'Thank you.'

As they turned towards the house, Sam lumbered to his feet and attempted to join them.

'No, you stay here with Hilary,' Jared said firmly. 'The last time I took you for a drive you barked all the time.'

'I expect he was excited,' Perdita offered.

'I'm sure you're right,' Jared agreed. 'But it didn't make it any less distracting.'

Napa was an attractive little place, sunny and colourful, with its open-air cafés and shops. Pulling into a parking lot, Jared stopped beneath the shade of a tree and led the way to a small but high class boutique with designer dresses in the window.

'You should get what you want here.'

It seemed dark inside after the brightness, and it took a moment or two for Perdita's eyes to adjust to the gloom.

A carefully made-up woman with hair dyed an unlikely shade of red came forward and, having assessed and approved Jared's look of affluence, enquired in a nasal drawl, 'May I help you?'

'We'd like to look at some swimwear.'

Apparently selling anything other than dresses was beneath her and the woman, clearly the manageress, signalled to a young assistant to serve them.

The girl, who hadn't taken her eyes off Jared since they'd walked in, came over eagerly and smiled at him.

Once more he took the lead. 'My wife would like to look at some swimwear.'

With a certain wry amusement, Perdita noted the flicker of disappointment and envy that the word *wife* had occasioned.

After asking her size, the girl produced a range of colourful, exotically patterned bikinis that were as brief as they were revealing.

Speaking to Perdita, but her eyes repeatedly straying to Jared, she said, 'You've sure got a great figure, so any of these should look good on you.'

Perdita was looking askance at the minute scraps of material when, indicating a white one-piece costume that was on a display stand, Jared said, 'Something more like this might fit the bill.'

'It's a Paul Gregor that's new in,' the girl told him, 'and luckily it's just the right size.'

Though apparently more modest, Perdita could see that the costume's daring cut would show off almost as much bare flesh as the bikinis and, feeling uncomfortable, she began, 'I really don't think—'

Cutting smoothly across her attempt to argue, Jared said to the girl, 'Then we'll take it,' and pulled out his wallet.

Unwilling to have him spend money on her, Perdita said sharply, 'If you insist on taking it, I'll buy it with my credit card. I don't want you to have to pay for it.'

'Darling…' A glint in his eye, he tilted her chin and kissed her thoroughly, lingeringly. 'You know quite well that I enjoy buying clothes for my wife.'

Shaken, her face flushed, Perdita stayed still and silent while the girl, who had been standing staring as though mesmerized came to life.

In a moment the swimsuit, which had an exorbitant price tag, had been paid for and the package handed to Jared.

'Thank you.' He returned the girl's smile.

Watching her visibly melt and give him a look that held both longing and an invitation, Perdita experienced a sudden swift pang of something that felt remarkably like jealousy.

No, surely she couldn't be jealous! She was annoyed with him, rocked by his kiss, but she couldn't be *jealous* just because he'd smiled at a shop assistant.

Yet she was.

When they reached the car he helped her in and, tossing the package onto the back seat, enquired, 'Do you fancy a relatively short sightseeing drive before I take you round the winery?'

With mingled emotions and still trying to regain her equilibrium, she hesitated for a moment before answering, 'Yes, that sounds lovely.'

A playful breeze tugging tendrils of silken hair free from its loose knot and flicking them against her hot cheeks, they took the scenic route north, driving in a leisurely way through St Helena and Rutherford, while Jared pointed out various things of interest.

When they reached the pleasant resort town of Calistoga, with its many local tourist attractions and hot springs, he brought the car to a halt outside a pretty little open-air café.

As they had tea beneath a fringed umbrella, glancing around, Perdita remarked, 'I really like this place; it's interesting and friendly.'

'I think you'll find the whole area is well worth another longer visit,' he agreed. 'Only a mile away is California's Old Faithful Geyser. It erupts every forty minutes or so and shoots a sixty-foot fountain into the air.'

Forgetting for a moment her reason for being here, she said enthusiastically, 'I'd love to see that.'

'Well, late autumn is a nice time to visit. Fewer holiday makers around.'

Autumn. It sounded very much as though he was expecting her to stay.

The realization kept her subdued and silent while they returned to the car and headed back south to the Wolf Rock Winery.

When they reached the entrance, he drove through tall wrought iron gates and drew up outside the main reception and sales area.

For some reason she had expected everything to look up to date and modern and she was surprised to find that the buildings were old-fashioned and elegant, more in the style of the French chateaux.

They appeared to be manned, however, mainly by Californian youths in cut-off jeans and flip-flops.

The contrast made Perdita smile.

When she had seen what there was to see, they left by the rear entrance. From there, partly hidden by a row of Spanish chestnuts, she could see the main bulk of the winery, with its huge external hoppers and enclosed conveyor belts.

Once inside, she found that if the reception buildings were old-fashioned, the winery itself was bang up to date with all the latest technology.

All the workers seemed open and friendly and, as they walked through the place, Jared greeted each man by name.

After a fascinating tour of the computer room and the fermentation rooms, with their huge stainless steel vats, Jared took her into the lab.

A tall, nice-looking man wearing a white coat and rimless glasses came to meet them. 'Hi, good to see you back,' he said cheerfully.

'Hi, Don. Good to *be* back,' Jared answered.

'Only the other day Estelle was saying it's about time you were home.'

'How is your wife?'

'She's fine, thanks.'

'When's the baby due?'

'In about six weeks.'

'Not long then before celebrations are in order.'

'I can't wait,' Don said fervently.

Putting an arm around Perdita's waist, Jared drew her forward. 'Darling, I want you to meet Don Macy, my chief oenologist and right-hand man... Don, this is my wife.'

Clearly surprised, Don said warmly, 'Nice to meet you, Mrs Dangerfield.'

Perdita had never been addressed as Mrs Dangerfield before and it threw her. But she managed to smile a greeting and they shook hands cordially.

'I hadn't realized you were married,' Don remarked to Jared. 'I take it congratulations are in order?'

Drawing Perdita closer, Jared answered, 'You could say that.'

Feeling her stiffen, he released her and changed the subject. 'What results have you had so far on that new project?'

'Quite good, though it doesn't show the same promise as Sunset Flight did at that stage...'

The two men talked wine for a minute or so before Perdita was shown over the lab, with its benches full of formidable-looking gadgetry.

She asked some pertinent and intelligent questions and, flattered by her interest in what he obviously considered one of the most satisfying jobs in the world, Don seemed only too delighted to explain the various procedures.

After some talk of pH levels, critical temperatures and chemical volatility, Jared asked, 'About ready to make a move?'

She nodded. 'If you are.'

Having thanked Don for his time and been assured that he'd enjoyed their visit, they made their way back to the car.

As Jared slid in beside her, he queried, 'You didn't find all that too boring?'

'Far from it,' she said with complete truth. 'In fact I would have liked to know more about the fermentation process.'

'Well, I'll be very happy to take you over whenever you want to go, though you'll find that one of the most exciting times is when the grapes have just been picked and are being unloaded...'

Once again he seemed to be taking it for granted that she would still be here later in the year.

When they drew up by the house, Jared suggested, 'Perhaps you'd care to go ahead and freshen up while I garage the car?'

As she made to get out, he reminded her, 'Don't forget your swimsuit.' With an ironic smile, he added, 'You might want to wear it.'

Still a little rattled by the way he had calmly ridden rough-shod over her, she had planned to leave it behind. But, unwilling to do battle, she picked it up reluctantly, her mouth set in a mutinous line, and saw by the gleam in his eyes that he was aware of, and amused by, her tacit rebellion.

When she reached her room she tossed the package on the bed, which had been neatly made, and feeling hot and sticky went through to the bathroom.

After a refreshing shower, she brushed her hair into a gleaming curtain before returning to the bedroom. Then, with absolutely no intention of following Jared's mocking suggestion, she found fresh undies and a sheath dress patterned in sea colours.

But a certain curiosity to see just what the swimsuit looked like on made her take it out of the box and try it.

It slipped on smoothly, seductively, and flowed over her slender curves like liquid honey.

There was no denying that it *felt* wonderful against her bare flesh, but what did it *look* like?

A glance in the long mirror sent a ripple of shock running through her.

The woman gazing back at her was slim as a willow wand, yet curvaceous, with shapely breasts, a narrow waist and nicely rounded hips.

Was that gorgeous creature really *her*? It was hard to believe that one single garment could make her look like that.

While she stared at herself, rooted to the spot, a movement in the mirror caught her eye. She became aware that the communicating door had opened and Jared was standing in the doorway, fully dressed, his hair still damp from the shower.

Spinning round, she demanded breathlessly, 'What are you doing in here?'

Eyes lingering on her delectable curves and long slender limbs, her silken hair and smooth skin, he answered almost reverently, 'Admiring a vision. When I last saw you, you were a lovely young girl; now you're a stunningly beautiful woman.'

Oddly moved, as much by the look on his face as by his words, she took refuge in anger. 'How dare you just walk in without knocking?'

'I did knock. You must have been too engrossed to hear.'

As her eyes fell, he added, 'There are drinks waiting on the terrace and I'd like you to join me.'

'I'll just take this off and—'

'Why not leave it on, and we'll have a quick swim before dinner?' Turning away, he closed the door quietly behind him.

No, she couldn't leave it on. She would feel too exposed, too vulnerable.

With unsteady hands she took off the swimsuit and thrust

it back into the box, before donning the undies and the blue-green sheath she had put ready earlier.

She was about to pin up her hair in the neat coil that Martin favoured when she recalled how Jared had once buried his face in it.

Her heart swelling, she let it fall in loose curls around her shoulders and, feeling oddly flustered, made her way through the cool, silent house to the hot, sunny terrace.

Sam came galumphing to meet her, nearly bowling her over in his excitement. 'Anyone would think you hadn't seen me for years,' she told him, laughing.

Jared looked up and said, 'Chickened out, I see.'

'I thought I'd better cover up. I've had enough sun for one day.'

Though clearly he recognized that as the excuse it was, he merely said, 'In that case you'd better come and sit in the shade.'

When she was settled in a lounger he tilted an umbrella to shield her from the sun which, though low in the sky, was still powerful.

As she looked up to thank him, his hand gentle, he stroked her hair. Then picking up a silky tendril and winding it around his finger, he remarked, 'I'm pleased to see you've left your hair down.' His voice sounded strangely husky.

A moment later, the huskiness gone, he queried politely, 'Now, what would you like to drink? A dry Martini? A gin and tonic? A fruit cocktail?'

'A fruit cocktail, please,' she answered.

While they sipped their drinks, the sun slipped below the horizon and the remaining brightness faded from the sky.

As the silence stretched, twilight began to drape perfumed veils, gauzy and insubstantial as a fairy's wings, over the garden. A solitary star shone brightly and the ghost of a thin crescent moon hung just above the treetops, promising yet another perfect summer evening.

But Perdita was unable to enjoy it.

In the past their silences had been warm, companionable, intimate, a quiet sharing of self, but since he had touched her hair so tenderly she had been tense, on edge, filled with a mixture of longing and doubt.

Uncomfortable with her own emotions, she wanted to break the silence but could think of nothing to say.

She found herself wondering if by any chance *his* feelings were following the same path as hers.

Flustered by the thought, she stared at the dusky slopes where lamps were being lit, while in the distance on the valley floor the highway they had driven down earlier that day was wearing a string of lights like a jewelled necklace.

The sight of the highway and the occasional arc of car headlights reminded her of their visit to the winery and, armed with a subject, she began, 'The wine Don Macy mentioned, Sunset Flight, was it...?'

'That's right. I'm surprised you remembered.'

'It's a lovely name and a memorable one, but it struck me that I've never heard it before.'

'No, you won't have done. It's a new rosé wine we're just launching. Don, who is a romantic at heart, named it.

'The grapes are a new variety we've been growing experimentally and, in order to produce something really special, we've tried marrying them with various other grape varieties. Don has put a great deal of time and skill into the project and, if he's got the balance right, which I believe he has, we should have a winner...'

He sounded relaxed, easy and after a moment or so her own tension began to drain away.

'As a matter of fact there's a bottle chilled and waiting to be opened,' he went on, 'so, when you're ready to eat, you can try some and tell me what you think of it.'

'I'm ready whenever you are.'

'If that's the case, I'll give Sam his supper and then we can make a start.'

Supper.

Watching him put the dog's bowl down, she thought that very soon her twenty-four hours would be up and he would want an answer.

But she was no nearer a decision.

How could she say yes and put herself in thrall to him once more?

Yet how could she say no and condemn her father to purgatory?

As Jared accompanied her to the table a thought struck her that made her feel hollow inside. If, in the end, she was forced to accept his proposition, how soon would he want her in his bed?

CHAPTER SEVEN

WHEN Jared removed the protective table cover Perdita saw that it had once again been set with linen napkins and crystal glasses.

But this time, as well as a candle, there was a beautiful centrepiece of fresh flowers and, in each of their places, an elaborate starter of crab claws and smoked salmon, while on a nearby trolley a range of silver dishes kept warm.

'It looks as though it's a special occasion,' she observed. 'A celebration.'

'It is.'

She waited for him to go on but, without elaborating, he pulled out her chair and seated her. Then, still standing, he lit the candle.

The sudden flare of light from beneath turned his handsome face into a mask, bringing some of his features to the fore and making black shadows in the hollows.

Sitting down opposite, he reached for a bottle of wine that stood in a cooler and, having opened it, he poured a glass and passed it to her.

The label, she saw, had the black silhouette of a graceful swallow-like bird soaring into an evening sky of palest pink and gold.

She lifted the glass and savoured the fragrant bouquet

before taking a sip. The wine was fresh and dry and smooth as silk, with a light delicate flavour and deeper undertones that she found extremely pleasing.

Taking another sip, she remarked, 'It's very distinctive. Though it's so smooth, it leaves just a hint of sparkle on your tongue. I don't recall ever having had anything quite like it before.'

'I agree it's very different. That's why I wanted to know what you thought of it.'

'I think it's lovely,' she said sincerely.

'Don believes it might eventually take its place alongside pink champagne as a wine that's perfect for birthdays and weddings and celebrations in general.'

The delicious taste still lingering, she said, 'I'm sure he's right.'

'Which makes it ideal for tonight.'

Having topped up her wine, he poured himself a glass and raised it in a toast. 'To us.'

A little uncertainly, she echoed, 'To us.' She took a sip before asking, 'So what is this special occasion? What are we celebrating?'

His lips twisted in a wry smile. 'I thought you might have guessed.'

But, even as she started to shake her head, she knew. Of course she did.

He was supremely confident that she would accept his proposition and go back to him.

Quivering inside, she waited until she was quite sure her voice would be steady before saying, 'Don't you think that, as I haven't yet given you an answer, your *celebration* may well be a little premature? I might say no.'

Candlelight gleamed in his eyes. 'I hope not. But, in any case, you've guessed wrongly.'

'Then what...?'

'I thought you might remember. Today is our third wedding anniversary…'

A shockwave ran through her. Of course. Usually she remembered only too well.

For the past two years, when the ninth of June came round she had struggled to push the knowledge and the memories to the back of her mind. Struggled to appear her normal well balanced self in front of her father and Martin, while all the old wounds reopened and she bled inwardly.

On this occasion, however, all the trauma, instead of reminding her, had somehow managed to crowd it out of her mind.

'And as this will be the first time we've spent our anniversary together,' he went on, 'a celebration seemed to be called for.

'Now, shall we start before Hilary's best culinary efforts are wasted?'

The starter, which proved to be delicious, was followed by melt-in-the-mouth chicken fillets stuffed with smoked oysters, tiny new potatoes, garden peas and a béchamel sauce. A dessert of raspberry shortcake and cream that was to die for made a fitting end to a special meal.

In spite of the lingering aftermath of shock, Perdita had enjoyed it and, when her plate was empty, she sat back with a sigh.

'Cheese?' Jared asked.

She shook her head. 'Just coffee, please.'

He rose to get it while she moved to sit in one of the comfortable loungers.

Out of range of the candlelight it was very nearly dark. Beyond the terrace the pool was as black as the Styx and on the crest of the hill the trees made inky silhouettes against the night sky.

When he reached the bar he touched a switch and the terrace, the patio and the pool area were lit by lanterns which gave the scene a romantic fairy tale appearance.

Returning with the coffee, he took a seat by her side and, stretching his long legs indolently, asked the question she had been dreading.

'So, have you made up your mind, Perdita?'

Shaking her head, she stammered, 'N-no, you'll need to be patient.'

His eyes on her face, he insisted, 'Considering everything, I think I've *been* patient. The twenty-four hours are up, and now I'd like an answer.'

'I can't give you one,' she cried in desperation. 'I just can't. I haven't had enough time to think.'

Which was rubbish and they both knew it.

'What is there to think about? You know as well as I do that you don't really have a choice.'

'But I have,' she insisted jerkily. 'I could always say no.'

His confidence in no way shaken, he asked, 'Could you really stand by and see your father made bankrupt and homeless?'

Her failure to answer answered for her.

'No, I didn't think you could.' His voice held the faintest hint of triumph. 'With his heart in the state it is, the strain might even kill him, and I'm sure you wouldn't want that on your conscience.'

'Whereas you *have* no conscience,' she flashed.

Jared shook his head. 'That's where you're wrong. As he's my father-in-law, I would much prefer not to have any part in his demise. However, knowing how much you love him, I'm quite sure that while you have the power to prevent it, you wouldn't put his life at risk. And of course it wouldn't only be your father who would suffer; there's your ex-fiancé and *his* father to think about.'

Hounded into a corner, she turned at bay. 'Neither my father, nor Martin, nor Elmer would want me to sacrifice myself.'

'How very melodramatic,' Jared said derisively.

'Mock all you like,' she cried, 'but if you honestly think I could come back to you and pretend to love you, you're mistaken.'

For an instant he looked as if she'd slapped him. Then, his face set, he said flatly, 'You misunderstand me. I don't want you to "pretend" to love me...'

As she stared at him, his eyes hard, his voice icy, he added, 'I really don't care a jot how you feel about me. All I want is you in my bed and available if I so much as lift a finger.'

'I was right,' she said shakily. 'You *are* crazy.'

'Then I prefer to be crazy with you *in* my life.'

'It w-would never work,' she stammered. 'If you still love me—'

'I don't...'

His denial hit her like a blow over the heart. She had foolishly imagined that, beneath all the anger and disillusionment, he still felt something for her other than mere lust.

'This is a purely physical thing,' he went on, rubbing it in, 'a kind of sickness, a fever in the blood, an obsession—give it any name you like. But, whatever you call it, I need you back in order to cure it, and I'm prepared to do whatever it takes to achieve that end. Luckily, I'm rich enough to be able to—'

'Buy me?' she flung at him.

'I was about to say, save your father's company, but if you prefer to put it that way...'

'That's what it amounts to.'

'So is your answer no?'

After a moment she said bitterly, 'You know perfectly well it has to be yes.'

'Don't look so desperate. It's not as if I'm asking you to do something you haven't done before, and very willingly, I might add.'

Her face flaming, she said, 'That was different.'

'In what way?'

'Then I loved you.'

He laughed harshly. 'You might have been in love with love, but never with me. If you'd really loved me you would have trusted me. Been willing to *listen* and believe me when I told you I was innocent. But instead you jumped to the conclusion that, because you had absented yourself on our wedding night, I'd either found a replacement or paid the nearest hooker—'

'How *could* I believe you when—' She broke off, biting her lip. 'Oh, what's the use of going through all that again?'

'None whatsoever while your mind is still so closed that you're unwilling to admit that there might be another explanation, rather than the obvious one, for what you saw.'

'I don't see how there can be,' she said, a stubborn set to her chin.

'There can be, and there is.'

'I wish I could believe you.'

'Well, whether you believe me or not, as you're my wife and I've waited three long years for this moment, I want you in my bed tonight.'

As she shivered, his eyes on her face, he continued softly, 'I want to feel your warm naked body against mine, I want to hear your moans as you writhe under me, I want to make love to you until you're begging for mercy and I'm completely sated.'

While she shuddered at his words, against her will she found herself aroused by them, and her heart began to race madly while a pool of molten heat formed low in the pit of her stomach.

As though he knew exactly what she was feeling, he asked softly, 'Does the idea turn you on?'

'No, it doesn't,' she denied hoarsely. 'I hate the very thought.'

'Your mind might hate the idea of you being naked and vulnerable in my arms, but I believe your body will love it.'

She knew only too well that what he said was true.

Taking a deep unsteady breath, she asked, 'How long would you want me…?'

'In my bed? For as long as it takes to finally get you out of my system.'

Her voice scarcely above a whisper, she asked, 'And then what?'

He shrugged as if it was of no consequence. 'When I've finished with you, Judson can have you back.'

She flinched at his deliberate cruelty.

'If he still wants my leftovers, that is.'

Flicked on the raw, she flashed, 'Why shouldn't he? You seem keen enough to have *his*.'

'I don't believe that you and he have ever been lovers,' Jared told her evenly.

Before she could respond, he suggested with blatant mockery, 'But perhaps he "respected" you too much to actually try?'

'Don't be ridiculous,' she snapped.

'Then how come you managed to keep him at bay?'

'I didn't do any such thing,' she denied.

But, though it had been subconscious, she had done exactly that. She had tended to regard Martin as a brother, think of him in a platonic way, rather than as a man with needs.

With that unnerving ability to read her mind, Jared pursued, 'Was his failure to stimulate your interest enough to dampen his ardour?'

The moment the words were spoken she realized how true they were, though until that minute she had been too grateful for Martin's restraint to question the reason for it.

Watching her face, Jared said with satisfaction, 'That appears to be right on the money.' Then, sounding genuinely puzzled, 'So if you don't really love him and he doesn't turn you on, what made you decide to marry him?'

'I *do* love him and he *does* turn me on—'

Seeing that Jared still looked unconvinced, she demanded, 'Do you seriously believe that Martin has remained celibate for nearly three years while he waited for me?'

'Why not? I have.'

She gaped at him, hardly able to credit it, yet hearing an unmistakable ring of truth in his voice.

Knocked sideways, needing to regain her equilibrium, she said, 'But, to finish answering your question, the main reason I decided to marry Martin was that I was sure I could trust him.'

The shot went home and she saw a flicker of pain and anger cross Jared's dark face before he asked, 'If you really believe that, why did it take you so long to agree to marry him?'

'Having made one bad mistake made me cautious.'

'And you didn't think that marrying Judson would be a mistake?'

'No. As I just said, I knew I could trust him.'

'Really?' Jared said shortly, 'Well, in answer to *your* question, no, I don't believe Judson has stayed celibate for three years while he waited for you. In fact I *know* he hasn't.'

'What do you mean?' she asked tightly.

'Though he's been very discreet about it, he keeps a mistress.'

'I don't believe you.'

'Then you should. She's a curvaceous blonde. Her name's Jackie Long and she has a flat in Olds Court, Fulham, which Judson pays for. He visits her there quite regularly.'

Badly shaken, Perdita said desperately, 'He *may* have done in the past, but I'm sure he hasn't since we got engaged.'

'That's where you're mistaken. He's been visiting his lady love just as regularly. He spent a couple of hours with her just before he flew to Japan.'

'You're lying!' she choked. But, even as she spoke, she knew he wasn't.

Though all she had ever felt for Martin was affection, the knowledge that he had been deceiving her knocked her completely off balance. She had believed in him implicitly, never for a moment suspecting that he had another woman.

But it might be partly *her* fault. If she'd agreed to marry him sooner…

Reading her thoughts with deadly accuracy, Jared said, 'A wife, especially an unworldly one, isn't necessarily enough for some men.'

Would that have applied to Martin?

Yesterday she would have said no with confidence. But now she was shaken to realize that she hadn't known him at all.

'Why so shocked?' Jared asked. 'Unless you had him down as some kind of saint?'

Perhaps, subconsciously, she had.

'If you did, to find he has feet of clay must be—'

Suddenly all the anger she felt was directed towards Jared. 'You're a fine one to take the moral high ground and stand in judgement!' she spat at him. 'Martin may not be perfect, but he wouldn't have taken another woman to bed on his wedding night.'

It was plain Jared didn't like that, but after a moment he let it go and said quietly, 'Neither did I. And it wasn't my intention to stand in judgement. I know from experience that three years is a long time, but after all the trouble he went to get you it seems…callow, lacking in self-control not to be prepared to wait…'

Then, clearly following a new and not too pleasant train of thought, 'You're a passionate woman so I can't rule out the fact that there may have been other men in *your* life before you got engaged to Judson.'

Still wanting to hit back, she said, 'Of course there were.' Then spoilt it by adding, 'Dozens.'

Jared's white teeth gleamed as he smiled wolfishly.

'Forgive me if I doubt that.' Then, consideringly, 'There's something about you, a kind of *innocence*, that makes me hope and believe you haven't had a lover since you left me.' A hardness to his voice, he went on, 'If I'm wrong and you *have*, then I'll just have to make you so completely mine again that you don't even remember what he looks like.'

Jumping to her feet, she walked blindly to the edge of the terrace and stood staring into space, his words burning into her brain.

It would have been bad enough if he had still loved her. But he didn't, so she would be just his plaything...

If she allowed herself to be.

But if she could stay cool and calm, freeze him off, she would be safe. He wouldn't force her, that was something she was certain of.

So she had the advantage.

Or had she? Would she be *able* to freeze him off?

In the past she had always found him irresistible, the chemistry between them immediate and potent. At one time he had only needed to touch her to reduce her to a state of abject desire. Indeed, he had been able to set her alight merely by *looking* at her in a certain way.

But that kind of response was long dead, she assured herself. After everything that had happened, only distrust and an unwilling attraction remained...

'Don't worry, it won't be all bad.'

Jared's voice from just behind her made Perdita jump a mile. She could feel the warmth of his breath on the back of her neck and, alarmed by how close he was, she had started to move away when he slid his arms around her and drew her back against him.

His lips brushing the side of her neck, making her shudder, he asked, 'About ready for bed?'

'No, I'm not at all tired,' she lied hoarsely.

'As sleep wasn't on the agenda, I'd prefer it if you weren't tired.'

The hardness had gone from his voice and now it was dangerously soft and seductive.

Gritting her teeth, she played for time. 'It's such a lovely night I'd like stay out here for a while.'

'Very well.' Taking her hand, he led her back to the nearest lounger and, stretching out, pulled her down into his arms.

The feel of his firm muscular body beneath hers made it hard to breathe and set her heart thumping so loudly she thought he must surely hear it.

Knowing it was useless to struggle and would only arouse him, she stayed quite still, stiff and unyielding and, in an attempt to distance herself mentally, stared fixedly at the lights reflected on the black surface of the swimming pool.

After a while the effort of holding herself so stiffly became too much and, she was forced to relax against him.

'That's better,' he remarked, and nuzzling aside her hair, touched his lips to the warmth of her nape.

Shivering, she tried to ignore that erotic caress but it set every nerve in her body tingling and she twisted a little in his arms.

As she did so, her breast brushed against his hand which had been lying idly across her ribcage.

His response was to stroke his thumb lightly over her nipple and he gave a little appreciative murmur when, beneath the thin silky material of her dress, it firmed to his touch.

Feeling an unwelcome heat spread through her, angry that her body had betrayed her so easily, she pulled herself free and scrambled to her feet.

He rose with her, smoothly and effortlessly and, slipping an arm around her waist, asked, 'Decided you'd like to go to bed after all?'

'No...' Her mind racing at top speed, she desperately sought a stay of execution. 'What I'd really like is a swim.'

'Be my guest.'

'I'll just—'

'There's no need to fetch your costume,' he broke in drily. 'The outside living area is well screened and private, even in daylight, and you'll find towels and robes in the changing cabins.'

As she hesitated, a taunt in his voice, he added, 'Don't forget I've seen you naked many times. However, if it bothers you, I promise I won't look.

'But, before you make your intention to swim obvious, I'd better put Sam to bed, otherwise he'll insist on joining you.'

She waited until the pair had vanished into the house before walking to the nearest cabin on legs that even now weren't quite steady.

Once inside, she stripped off her clothes and, leaving them on the bench, pulled on one of the towelling robes that hung from a row of hooks.

Seeing no sign of Jared, when she reached the edge of the pool she draped the robe over one of the nearby sunbeds and, descending the steps, slipped into the water.

It was blissfully cool and felt like satin against her bare skin. After swimming a couple of lengths she turned to float on her back, motionless, her hair fanning out around her like bright seaweed.

The night was silky dark and quiet apart from the endless shrill song of the cicadas. The sky above her head was a vault of black velvet, the stars closer than she had ever seen them before.

When she had looked her fill she turned and swam to the side. She was on the point of getting out when she realized that Jared had returned, and started to swim another length.

It was years since she'd done any serious swimming and after ten or twelve lengths she would have been pleased to stop. But, unready to face what would happen once she left the pool, she forced herself to keep going until common sense told her she was being a fool. She couldn't keep swimming all night.

Making her way to the steps, she started to climb them, shocked to discover how leaden her limbs felt.

Jared appeared and held out a hand to help her.

'Tired?' he asked.

'A little,' she admitted.

He reached for the towelling robe she had discarded earlier and wrapped it around her.

'In that case…' Taking her hand, he led her towards the jacuzzi.

It was screened from the house and terrace by a waist-high semicircular stone wall, but the front was open to what in daylight would be a pleasant view over the gardens.

As they approached, Perdita could hear the faint bubbling sound of water and see wisps of steam rising from the surface. A nearby alcove held a neat pile of towels.

Slipping the robe from her shoulders, he said, 'This is what you need.'

A broad seat made a horseshoe round the tub and when she had descended the steps she sat down, submerged up to her shoulders.

The gentle erotic swirl of hot water around her weary limbs felt lovely and she was just starting to relax when Jared enquired, 'Mind if I join you?'

Her breath caught in her throat, she said nothing.

He stripped off his clothes and a moment or two later sat down by her side, a great deal too close for comfort.

Knowing that if she moved a fraction his naked thigh would brush against hers, she sat quite still.

After a moment he remarked softly, 'You're as taut as a drawn bowstring. Why don't you loosen up and let the water do its work?'

Seeing the sense of that, she made a great effort to follow his advice.

The last forty-eight hours had been highly charged and had taken their toll. But, after a while, lulled by the warmth of the water, her tired body massaged by the jets, she managed to relax and, closing her eyes, let herself drift.

She was roused by a mouth touching hers and a voice saying gently, 'It seems a shame to disturb you, but it's time we were moving.'

Alarmed by that kiss, she scrambled up and, losing her footing, would have slipped if Jared hadn't caught her arms and steadied her.

'Careful now. You're still half asleep.'

An arm at her waist, he saw her safely up the steps and draped the robe loosely about her shoulders, before fastening a towel around his own lean hips.

As he picked up another towel, realizing his intention and scared stiff of what it might do to her, she said sharply, 'Don't touch me.'

'What's wrong?' He sounded genuinely surprised.

Afraid that if he touched her she would be lost, incapable of freezing him off, she said, 'I don't want you to touch me.'

Though his face gave nothing away, she felt sure she had vexed him. Perhaps if she made him angry enough he'd give up and leave her alone, for the time being, at least.

Guessing that the mention of Martin would be like a red rag to a bull, she lied, 'I've got used to Martin touching me.'

Seeing Jared raise a derisive brow, she ploughed on, 'He may be no saint but, contrary to what you seem to think, he's always been able to give me everything I need.'

His voice as smooth as silk, Jared said, 'Don't worry. I'm sure I can do the same.'

'I very much doubt it,' she told him recklessly. 'In any case, I don't fancy being pawed by a man I don't love.'

The look on his face told her that not only had she succeeded in making him angry, but his certainty that she didn't love Martin and hadn't slept with him had been badly shaken.

That look was gone in an instant and, his voice calm, dispassionate, he said, 'While you may prefer Judson's attentions, from now on you'll have to put up with mine.'

The big towel he held was soft and absorbent, his touch gentle as he proceeded to dry her off; even so, every nerve in her body zinged into life when he drew her back against him and began to rub her hair.

That done, he dried her throat and shoulders and her firm breasts while, his lips brushing her ear, he whispered, 'Do you remember the last time we shared a jacuzzi? How, afterwards, we drank red wine and made love under the stars...?'

Oh, yes, she remembered that perfect night, remembered how they had stretched out on his swingseat and shared some of the sweetest lovemaking she had ever known.

Though she tried to close her mind to the poignant memories, tried to distance herself, her limbs grew heavy and languorous and warmth spread through her.

She was aware of both their heartbeats and the way his breaths fell between her own, achingly alive to the brush of his skin against hers and the firmness of his muscles, conscious of every bone in his body.

It was an awareness so intense, so all consuming that it seemed to take over her entire being. She wanted to turn to him, put her arms around his neck and let her body melt against his.

No, she thought, making an attempt at a last-ditch stand, she mustn't allow herself to be seduced so easily, mustn't let him know that his strategy was succeeding.

But his closeness and the memories it engendered were so piercingly sweet that she found it almost impossible to hide what she was feeling, hide her growing longing.

And he knew.

Turning her into his arms, he began to kiss her softly, her lips, her temples, her closed eyelids, the long line of her throat and the warm hollow at the base.

She waited impatiently for him to reach her breasts, where the firm nipples ached for the touch of his mouth and tongue.

When he finally reached his goal and began to suckle sweetly, first one and then the other, tugging a little, repeatedly teasing the sensitive tip with his tongue, she shivered at the exquisite sensations he was arousing.

When she began to make little sounds deep in her throat, he slid his free hand slowly down the length of her body, past the slim waist and over the smooth skin of her abdomen, to the nest of pale silky curls between her thighs.

Any attempt at resistance swamped by a surge of burning desire, she held her breath.

But his hand stilled and he asked softly, 'Do you want me to stop, Perdita?'

She shook her head.

As though unconvinced, he remarked, 'Earlier you said you didn't want to be pawed by a man you didn't love.'

'I didn't mean it.'

'So you *do* want me to go on?'

'Yes.'

'Sure?'

Still on fire, she begged hoarsely, 'Please, oh, please, Jared.'

'Is lover boy able to make you feel like this, able to make you beg and plead?'

His words shocked her into awareness and, opening dazed eyes, she looked up into his face. There was a cruel twist to his lips and he looked both satisfied and triumphant.

In that instant she realized with a kind of sick panic that he hated her. He had been playing with her, not to give her pleasure and release, but to pay her back for the things she had said, to mortify her and drive home his absolute mastery.

She felt shamed, humiliated.

Adrenalin pumping through her veins, she stepped back and dashed his hand away.

A slight smile on his lips, he looked down at her.

That smile was the last straw.

Lifting her hand, she cracked it across his face with every last ounce of her strength, then turned and ran.

CHAPTER EIGHT

HER legs feeling curiously stiff and alien, her breath coming in shallow gasps, Perdita fled through the silent house.

When she reached her room she fumbled for the light switch and, fearing pursuit, banged the door shut behind her and turned the key. Remembering the communicating door, she hurried to wedge a chair beneath the handle.

Then, not bothering with the night dress that lay ready on the bed, she crept beneath the duvet and turned off the lamp.

Jared hated her...

Huddled there, she gave way to the unbearable pressure that had built up inside and cried as though her very heart would break.

How could a man who had once sworn he loved her treat her in such a way?

But, even while the scalding tears flowed and the sobs that racked her took more breath than she had, a basic honesty made her admit that she was at least partly to blame. She had taunted him about Martin, angered him deliberately.

A dangerous thing to do to a man like Jared.

She heard the sound of a door handle being tried and, despite the sobs still rising in her throat, held her breath, afraid that he would be furious enough to break in.

But there wasn't another sound and, turning her face into

the pillow, she let the bitter tide of anguish and grief wash over her once more.

Jared hated her...

Swamped by misery almost too great to be borne, she hadn't heard him come in and the first she knew of his presence was when a gentle hand touched her still-damp hair.

Gasping with shock, she flinched and, through her tears, demanded, 'How did you get in?'

'By way of the veranda.'

'Go away; I don't want you here,' she cried hoarsely.

Ignoring her words, he discarded the short silk robe he was wearing and slid into bed beside her. Then, drawing her to him, he held her close and stroked her hair while he murmured inarticulate words of comfort.

Making an effort to pull herself together, she tried to stop the flow of tears but his unexpected tenderness only made them flow faster.

She cried for lost dreams and shattered hopes, for the love that she had once believed was hers, for the hard, bitter man Jared had become, and for what *might* have been. Cried until there were no tears left and shuddering breaths took the place of the sobs.

Jared cradled her to him and, reaching for the box of tissues on the bedside cabinet, pulled out a handful and dried her wet face. Then, settling her head on his shoulder, he said softly, 'Try and get some sleep now.'

Physically and emotionally spent, she let go her grip on consciousness and almost immediately slept.

Sometime towards morning she began to dream, a bright, vivid dream of a lovely summer's day.

Sam, ears flapping and looking utterly ridiculous, was galumphing about chasing an elusive butterfly while she lay cradled in Jared's arms in the hammock slung from a sturdy branch beneath the cedar tree. Dappled sunlight coming through the canopy of leaves fell warmly on their faces and they breathed in the scent of newly mown grass carried on the light balmy breeze.

She could feel the flesh and bone and muscle of Jared's body next to hers, the slight rise and fall of his chest, the strong beat of his heart.

All his hardness, his anger had vanished as if it had never been and he was once again the warm, charismatic man she had met and married.

Love for him overwhelmed her and, with a little murmur of gladness, she nestled against him.

When his arms tightened around her and she lifted her face to his, he kissed her softly until her lips parted beneath the sweetness of that kiss.

His mouth moving against hers was all she had ever wanted or needed and, her arms sliding around his neck with a little murmur of pleasure, she kissed him back.

It wasn't until his hands began to travel over her naked body that she surfaced sufficiently to realize that this was no dream.

Rather than lying in a hammock in the sun, they were lying in her bed in the grey light of very early morning and Jared was no longer the old loving Jared of her dream, but the cold, hard man who had deliberately set out to humiliate her.

She stiffened and made an attempt to pull away.

But, whispering, 'It's all right, my love, it's all right,' he drew her to him and held her close. 'I'm sorry I was such a brute to you. Forgive me.'

While panic and need and reason warred inside her, he stroked her hair and whispered soft words of reassurance and comfort.

Only when he felt her relax against him did his hands begin to move over her once more, stroking and caressing her breasts with seductive skill.

While his fingers found and teased one velvety nipple, he bent his head and his lips explored her jaw line and the soft skin beneath until they reached the base of her throat and lingered there, sending shivers running through her.

Then his mouth moved lower and closed over the other nipple, while her heart began to throw itself against her ribs and her pulse raced out of control.

As she gasped, pierced by needle-sharp darts of pleasure, the fingers of his free hand slid down to the warm skin of her inner thighs and buried themselves in the silky curls.

Finding his goal unerringly, he began to delicately explore the slick warmth that awaited there.

As those long fingers moved inside her, bringing their promise of delight, any semblance of control began to slip from her grasp.

Lost and mindless, she was on the point of abandoning her body to its fate when, even through the haze of passion, she felt a fresh surge of fear and stiffened.

Instantly he was aware of it. Raising his head, he said softly, 'Relax. I promise I won't hurt you or do anything you don't want me to do.'

He kissed her and after a moment or two she let go of the panic and opened her mouth to his kiss.

When she was once again lying in his arms, relaxed and pliant, he brought her to a new peak of wanting before turning her onto her back. Then, while his mouth claimed hers, he lowered himself into the waiting cradle of her hips.

But, even then, as though wanting to be certain how she felt, he held back.

When, the previous evening, he had told her that he'd been celibate for the past three years, she had believed him, and now she found herself marvelling at his self-control.

Roused to fever-pitch herself and hoping his abnormal restraint wouldn't last too long, she moved her hips in a tacit invitation as old as Eve, and felt the jerk of his body's instant response.

But, even then, he paused to ask, 'Do you want me to make love to you, Perdita?'

She nodded.

'I want to hear you say it,' he insisted. 'Do you want me?'

'Yes, yes…' she whispered urgently.

A moment later a shudder that was a mixture of relief, gladness and passion shook her and, as he started to move and she gave herself to him, her body began to hum with sheer delight.

She was caught up by a heated tide of feeling, the like of which she hadn't experienced for over three years, where past and future ceased to exist and there was only the here and now.

Racked by the most incredible pleasure, all she could do was cling on and ride wave upon wave until finally she was washed onto the shore, where she lay spent and shattered, like a survivor of some catastrophic force of nature.

Jared's head was heavy on her breast and she could feel his heart still thundering against her.

As her own heartbeat and breathing gradually slowed to something approaching normal, she made an effort to gather herself.

At the same time Jared raised his head and lifted himself away. Then, a hand softly stroking her cheek, his voice full of tenderness and concern, he asked, 'All right?'

Opening heavy eyelids, she looked up into his dark, handsome face.

She nodded mutely, then finding her voice, whispered, 'Wonderful.'

An expression of pure male satisfaction appeared on his face that she found oddly moving.

'That's good,' he told her softly, 'because we've a lot of

catching up to do, and in a little while I intend to make love to you all over again.'

If that first time had been wonderful, the lovemaking that followed was indescribable. Like someone who had been too long denied, Jared made love to her not twice, but several times. Varied and inventive lovemaking that left her limp and quivering and totally blissful.

Each time, when she thought herself sated, with deftness and skill and the sure knowledge of how the female body worked, he was able to re-coil that spiral of desire and bring her to yet another shuddering climax.

When even his amazing stamina was finally eroded, he stretched out beside her and, cradling her in his arms, settled her head at the comfortable junction between chest and shoulder.

After a short time, when his breathing grew light and even and his hold loosened slightly, easing herself away a little, she studied his face.

In the early morning light she could see that his eyes were closed, the heavy lashes fanning out on his hard cheeks. With his firm mouth relaxed in sleep and some of the lines of pain smoothed away, he looked younger, more carefree, almost like the Jared of old.

Since he had taken her in his arms and dried her tears, she had seen no sign of the hard, cruel man who had deliberately humiliated her.

Though a masterful lover, he'd been kind and generous, careful and heartbreakingly tender, and after three long years in the wilderness she knew what it was to feel like a woman again.

Just at the moment she could think no further ahead than that.

Tiredness washing over her, she settled herself once more and in response to that slight movement his arm tightened around her possessively.

* * *

When she awoke it was broad daylight, the muslin curtains were stirring a little in the slight breeze from the open windows and the room was filled with fresh air and sunshine.

She was alone in the bed. There was no sign of Jared but the door between their two bedrooms was standing open.

While her body felt sleek and contented, her brain seemed to be stuck in neutral, unable, or unwilling, to engage or function properly.

Sitting up in bed, she listened. Faintly, in the background, were what she was starting to recognize as the normal sounds of the Valley, while closer at hand she could hear a shower running and a low tuneful whistling.

Then the water and the whistling stopped and a moment or two later Jared appeared in the doorway, stark naked and still towelling his dark hair.

She had a few seconds to feast her eyes on him before he realized she was awake and watching him. He looked happy, she thought, almost carefree, more like the man she had known and loved.

He also looked so stunningly attractive, so very male, that the breath caught in her throat and her heart rate soared.

At that moment he glanced up and, seeing she was awake, gave her that slow smile he had always reserved solely for her.

'I came to see if you were awake and ready to eat but if you keep looking at me like that brunch might have to wait.' Blushing a little, she tore her gaze away.

Strolling over to the bed, the towel draped around his neck, he stood looking down at her.

Suddenly conscious of her unwashed state and the fact that her hair was a tangled mass of rats tails and her eyes were probably still swollen, she said, 'I must look an absolute fright.'

'You've always looked beautiful first thing in the morning,' he told her softly. 'Fresh and sweet and utterly enchanting.

Now, all tousled and inviting and still flushed with sleep, you look irresistible.'

He stooped to give her a lingering kiss.

Through the haze of pleasure that engulfed her, she smelled the clean fresh scent of toothpaste and shower gel and aftershave all mingled together and felt the slight dampness of his skin.

'Mmm...' he murmured against her lips. Then, without regret, 'Brunch will have to wait after all.'

As he slid back into bed and pulled her down into his arms, she made a half-hearted protest. 'But what about your housekeeper? Suppose she came in and found us like this—'

He stopped the words with a kiss before saying, 'Hilary will be busy in the kitchen... And, in any case, as a respectable married couple, we're quite entitled to be in bed together.'

They made love more than once and ended up sharing a shower, so it was some considerable time later that, finally dressed for the day, they wended their way out on to the sunny terrace to break their fast.

Perdita had been so engrossed by *feelings* that it wasn't until they were sitting opposite each other beneath the partial shade of an umbrella that a shaft of bright sunlight falling across his face made her draw in her breath sharply.

Seeing where her eyes were fixed, he lifted a hand and touched his left cheek where, high on the cheekbone, there was a dull red mark and the beginnings of a bruise.

'I did that?' she breathed, aghast.

'It's where your ring caught me.' His voice was easy, matter-of-fact.

Her eyes filled with tears. 'I'm sorry,' she whispered huskily.

He leaned across the table and took her hand. 'Don't be upset. I deserved it.'

Then, looking at the wide chased-gold ring she wore on the

middle finger of her right hand, a sudden edge to his voice, he asked, 'Did Judson give you this?'

She shook her head. 'No. It was a twenty-first birthday present from Dad.'

As he moved the ring round with his thumb in an attempt to read the ornate letters engraved on it, she told him, 'It just says Perdita.'

'Lost lady,' he murmured softly. Reaching for the coffee pot, he added, 'You've never told me why you were called Perdita.'

'It's a long story.'

'We've got all day—' he gave her hand a squeeze and released it before pouring the coffee '—so start from the beginning.'

When she had taken a sip, she began, 'My mother came from San Jose. Dad met her when he went out to California to help establish the American side of Judson Boyd Electronics.

'It was love at first sight and within a matter of weeks they were married. They bought a house and set up home there, not far from where Elmer lives now.

'When my mother was seven months pregnant, my father, who absolutely adored her, took her on a long-promised visit to New York.

'The evening before they were due to fly back to California, she went into premature labour and had to be rushed into Rodanth Hospital.

'There were complications and, while I was put in the premature baby unit, they struggled to save her life. It was touch and go and for twenty-four hours Dad never left her side.

'When she finally regained consciousness fully and asked to see her baby, I couldn't be found and she and Dad were warned that I might have died.

'But, the following morning, when they were both in despair, I was discovered at Tidewell, a subsidiary of Rodanth where, due to a mix-up of names, I'd been sent by mistake.

'The error came to light when a Mrs Boyt, who had been transferred to Tidewell after giving birth to a little boy, was presented with a daughter. Apparently the poor woman had hysterics, but things were soon put right and she got her son back safely, while I was returned to my parents.'

'Hence the name, Perdita,' Jared finished for her. Then, gently, 'What happened to your mother?'

'They hadn't succeeded in stopping the internal bleeding, and she died the next day while Dad held her in his arms...

'Elmer once told me that Dad never got over her death, that it was as if part of him died with her.

'He took me back to California and hired a nanny to help take care of me. But he'd only stayed in the States because of my mother, and he couldn't settle without her. So he sold the house and everything in it and returned to England to run the British side of the company...'

'Are you very like your mother?'

'The image of her, apparently.'

'And you were all he had left,' Jared said thoughtfully. 'That explains a great deal.'

She seized the opportunity to say out loud one of the things that had been nagging at her. 'The fact that Dad *does* think so much of me makes it almost impossible to tell him...' She hesitated.

'That you've been coerced into coming back to me?' Jared asked a shade bitterly.

'Yes,' she admitted.

'So what *are* you going to tell him?'

'I'm not sure,' she said. 'Certainly not the whole truth. And I'm scared stiff that either he or Martin might ring me before I've made up my mind just what to say.'

'Then I suggest it would make sense to forestall them both by calling them first.'

'But what am I to tell them?'

'If you want to buy time, tell them the negotiations are going well and you have every hope of success, but that it might be several days yet before any firm agreement is reached. When it is, you'll let them know at once…'

Though she knew it was only putting off the evil day, she seized on the suggestion. At the very least, it should help to put her father's mind at rest and prevent him worrying.

'But this afternoon,' Jared went on, 'I was planning to take you to see the Petrified Forest—'

'Oh, I've heard of it. Isn't that where, because of a volcanic eruption that occurred millions of years ago, giant redwoods have been preserved?'

'That's the place, and it's a longish trip…' Reaching for the outdoor phone, he passed it across to her. 'So it might make sense to phone them before we start. If my calculations are right, it'll be evening in London and breakfast time in Tokyo, so with a bit of luck you should catch them both. Don't forget you're supposed to be in New York,' he added, 'where it's mid-afternoon.'

Anxious to get it over, Perdita rang her father first and, when she heard his voice, said quickly, 'Hi, Dad… Just thought I'd let you know…'

Having repeated almost word for word what Jared had suggested and heard him breathe, 'Thank the Lord,' she asked how he was.

'Not bad at all,' he said cheerfully. 'In fact I've been told I can go home in a day or two.'

'That's really great news, so long as you take good care of yourself.'

'Sally's promised to look after me, and only bully me when it's for my own good.

'But what about you? Though you're obviously spending a lot of time talking, I hope you're managing to get out and about a bit?'

'Oh, yes, as a matter of fact I'll be going out as soon as I've talked to Martin.'

'I'll tell Sally. She seems a bit concerned about you. Every time she comes in to see me she asks if I've heard from you.'

'Well, tell her not to worry, everything's fine.'

When, after they had said their goodbyes, she ended the call, Jared queried, 'Sally?'

'Yes. Dad says she seems a bit concerned about me.'

'It was nice of you to reassure her.'

'I'm getting quite good at lying,' she said. Then, seeing Jared's quick frown, wished she hadn't rocked the boat.

Only too conscious of the gulf that now yawned between herself and Martin, the call she made to him was even more stressful.

Having told him what she had told her father, asked how things were at his end and been assured that they were going reasonably well and he should be home any day now, she could hardly wait to get away.

Sounding more than a little put out, he observed, 'You seem to be in a hurry.'

'I'm on the point of going out,' she told him, 'but, in case I don't get another chance to talk to you today, I wanted to do it before I went.'

'I'm sorry.' He sounded contrite. 'It's just that I'm missing you like hell.'

He was probably missing his mistress even more, she thought caustically.

'Still, with a bit of luck,' he went on, 'you'll be home before too long with a good result.'

'I hope so.' Then, quickly, 'Well, I really must go. 'Bye.'

'Love you.'

She smiled bitterly. He sounded as if he meant it.

'You don't look any too happy,' Jared remarked as she handed him back the phone.

Once again, she found herself taking her anger and disillusionment out on him. 'You think it's easy having to sit here and lie to...the man I love.'

Jared's face darkened. 'Then you still love him?'

'Of course I still love him. He may be far from perfect, but two wrongs don't make a right, and I feel guilty about deceiving him.'

'You didn't seem to feel guilty earlier, when we were in bed together.'

Wanting to hit back, she said, 'What I feel guilty about is encouraging Martin to believe everything's all right when it isn't...' Then, dismissively, 'When we were in bed together it was much the same as Martin visiting his mistress—just sex.'

For one brief unguarded moment Jared looked as if she'd kicked him in the solar plexus, then a shutter came down. 'And that was all it was?'

'It was all you said you wanted from me, and sex alone means very little.'

'It seemed to mean a great deal to you three years ago in Las Vegas...'

'That's all in the past,' she said desperately.

But, as though she hadn't spoken, he went on, 'It seemed to mean a great deal to you when you destroyed everything there was between us just because you thought I'd taken another woman to bed.'

'I didn't *think* you had. I *knew* you had. I can't imagine that many men take a woman, other than their wife, to bed on their wedding night.'

'I can't imagine that many men are left alone on their wedding night.'

'And that's your excuse?'

'No, I don't need an excuse. I never so much as *looked* at another woman that night. Or any other night, for that matter. As far as I was concerned, once I met you no other woman existed.'

She *wanted* to believe him. But how could she?

'However, as you keep telling me, that's all in the past. No longer important. We've moved on, and all that's left is lust...'

Shaken to her very soul, she longed to deny his words but, as she had been the first to say it, how could she?

'So, for the time being at least,' he went on, 'that will have to be enough.

'Now, are you about ready to go?' He sounded brisk, matter-of-fact, as if he had accepted the emptiness of their relationship and decided that it really didn't matter.

Still his grey eyes held a bleakness that made her want to cry, and her heart felt like lead as she allowed herself to be escorted out to the car.

Over the next two or three days, as though they had tacitly agreed a truce, they were both careful never to say a word out of place.

But, although Jared was always scrupulously polite and mindful of her comfort and well-being, there was never any feeling of closeness.

Part of him stayed aloof and remote, as though he had mentally distanced himself, while Perdita found she was trapped in a kind of limbo. A prisoner who was waiting, without quite knowing what she was waiting for.

The only time she could escape for a while was at night when she closed her eyes and her mind and abandoned herself to Jared's passionate, sometimes almost fierce, lovemaking.

But, in spite of the intense physical pleasure he gave her, afterwards, when she lay in his arms, she always felt strangely empty, incomplete, as if something fundamental and necessary was lacking.

Each morning, given the option of either idling by the pool

or going out sightseeing, things being as they were, she chose the latter.

One day they visited Sonoma and, on another, they drove all the way to Clear Lake. Then the following day they walked one of the many scenic trails in the Robert Louis Stevenson State Park on the slopes of Mount St Helena.

But, even when their days were fully occupied, Perdita had the feeling that she was trapped in some kind of time warp, unable to either retreat or go forward, where very little was how it seemed and nothing was quite real.

While her father phoned only once to tell her he was now home, Martin, who was back in London, showed every sign of becoming restive. As though he'd picked up the fact that everything wasn't as it should be, he had phoned almost every day.

Each time he had asked her if she loved him and if everything was all right, forcing her to either lie or prevaricate, and causing Jared's face to grow hard and set as he listened to her stumbling replies.

On the last occasion, having replaced the phone, she said raggedly, 'I can't go on like this... But neither can I bring myself to tell him and Dad how things are...'

His voice even, Jared suggested, 'I thought you might have come to terms with the idea by now?'

'Well, I haven't.'

'Is it really going to be so impossible to tell them that everything's all right? To explain that we were married in Las Vegas and we're still legally man and wife?'

'I can tell them we're married, but how can I pretend that everything's all right when they both know I would never willingly live with a man I couldn't trust?'

A white line appearing round his mouth, Jared said, 'It always comes back to that, doesn't it?'

There was such a look of despair on his face, such bitter

desolation, that she longed to take back those words, to try and make things right between them.

But it was too late, she recognized hopelessly. Nothing would make things right between them. He no longer loved her. As he had said, all that was left was anger and bitterness and lust.

As she sat in stricken silence, he changed the subject and for the rest of the day when they talked it was stiltedly, like a couple of adversaries forced into an unlikely truce.

That night when she went to bed, instead of accompanying her he stayed on the terrace and, hours later, still lying alone, Perdita shed silent tears.

Nothing could alter the past, she knew, and as it was, things would never be right between them.

It was a long time before she finally fell asleep.

When she awoke, it was to find that she was still alone in the big bed, and an undented pillow made it clear that Jared hadn't even slept beside her.

For the past three or four mornings he had kissed her awake and they had showered together, but now the door between their rooms was closed.

Heavy-hearted she got out of bed and went to shower and brush her teeth before returning to the bedroom to dress.

Hilary, an amiable, fair-haired woman in her late forties, was quietly efficient, and freshly laundered clothes and underwear had been replaced neatly in the wardrobe, giving Perdita plenty of choice.

When she had put on clean undies and a light cotton dress, she fastened her gleaming flaxen hair loosely in the nape of her neck and made her way out to the sunny terrace, where Sam was waiting to give her his usual enthusiastic welcome.

There was still no sign of Jared, and Hilary was bringing out breakfast before he appeared, looking heartbreakingly handsome in well-cut trousers and an open-necked sports shirt.

He exchanged pleasantries with the housekeeper and, having fended off Sam's boisterous greeting, took a seat at the table and reached to pour the coffee.

When Hilary had disappeared kitchenwards, his expression cool and guarded, giving nothing away, he turned to Perdita and enquired with distant civility, 'I hope you slept well?'

'Very well, thank you,' she lied. And wondered with a sinking heart how she was going to get through the day. It had been bad enough previously, but now, faced with this polite stranger, it was an even more daunting prospect.

They were just finishing what had proved to be an almost silent meal when Jared's cellphone rang.

'Hello?...' he answered crisply. Then, 'Yes, of course. I'll be along as soon as I've finished my coffee... Yes, we can manage that... Yes, I'm sure she will. It should be a nice change... Right, see you shortly.'

Dropping the phone back into his pocket, he remarked, 'That was Don. It seems I'm needed over at the winery. The problem should be sorted out by mid-morning at the latest, then Don and Estelle have invited us to a lunchtime barbecue. It'll give you an opportunity to meet some of the people who live in the Valley.'

Carefully, she said, 'That should be nice.'

'In the meantime, do you mind being left alone?'

'No, not at all,' she assured him. In many ways it would be a relief.

'Then I'll see you in an hour or so.'

He had started to walk towards the garage block when he half turned to mention casually, 'By the way, after the barbecue we'll be taking a trip, so while I'm gone it might be a good idea to pack a few things. I've asked Hilary to find you a smallish case.'

A little puzzled by this sudden decision, Perdita asked, 'Where are we going?'

'Las Vegas for a day or two.'

'Las Vegas?' she echoed, aghast. 'Why?'

'Trying to ignore the past hasn't worked, so I think it may be time to confront it.'

He was turning to go when he paused to say, 'By the way, include something suitable for the evenings. We may need to dress up.'

Feeling hollow inside, Perdita stared after him. The last thing she wanted to do was go to Las Vegas. It held too many unhappy memories. Memories she had struggled for the past three years to leave behind.

But now it seemed that, rather than leaving them behind, Jared was determined to go and face them.

CHAPTER NINE

WHEN Perdita had watched Jared drive away, she went through to her room and began to put her clothes in neat piles on the bed.

The only thing she had with her suitable for evenings was a black cocktail dress. With it she put a pair of strappy sandals, an evening purse and the velvet-covered box that contained her small amount of jewellery.

As she did so her mind went back to the last time she had packed to go to Las Vegas. Then she had been living in Elmer's house in San Jose, and her hands had been eager, her thoughts happy and full of anticipation.

That happiness had been dimmed somewhat when Martin, whom she had presumed would still be at work, had suddenly appeared in the hall just as she was coming down the stairs with her case.

Earlier, she had written a brief note to leave for him, explaining that she was spending 'a long weekend away with a friend'.

Looking upset and agitated, he had blocked her way, demanding, 'Where do you think you're going?'

'That's absolutely nothing to do with you,' she retorted sharply.

'If you're sneaking out to—'

'I'm not *sneaking out*. I don't need to sneak. I haven't anything to hide.'

'If you haven't anything to hide, tell me where you're going.'

'I'm going to Las Vegas with a friend.'

'Jared Dangerfield, I suppose.'

'You suppose right.'

'I can't let you do it.'

'You can't stop me. I'm not a child any longer. I'm old enough to do exactly as I please. In any case, it's none of your business.'

'Before your father went into hospital I promised him I'd keep an eye on you.'

'Spy on me, you mean!'

'I'm only trying to take care of you. You don't know what you're doing—'

'I know exactly what I'm doing, so will you please get out of my way?'

'If you insist on leaving I'll have no option but to tell your father.'

Chin up, she faced him squarely and said, 'I'm going, and if you tell Dad and worry him at a time like this, I'll never forgive you. *Never.*'

Seeing she meant it, he resorted to pleading. 'Please, Dita, listen to sense—'

But, hearing Jared's car, she made an attempt to brush past him.

He caught her wrist and said urgently, 'At least tell me where you're staying.'

'We're staying at the Imperial Palace.'

'Yes. I know it, so if by any chance I need to get hold of you—'

'As I have every intention of keeping in touch with the hospital myself, you should have no need to get hold of me.'

Pulling free, she hurried out.

Jared met her on the doorstep and, after a quick kiss, stowed her case next to his own, before helping her into the front passenger seat.

Turning her head, she caught a glimpse of Martin watching them from the window, his face contorted with anger and a kind of helpless concern.

As they left San Jose behind them and headed south, Perdita took her engagement ring from her locket and slipped it onto her finger.

Showing he never missed a thing, Jared asked, 'Does wearing that make you feel a little less guilty about this weekend?'

She said, 'I don't feel guilty,' and knew he didn't believe her.

The truth was, he knew her better than she knew herself. Though she had eventually managed to push any feelings of guilt to the back of her mind, Martin's well intentioned intervention had brought them to the fore again.

She sighed, regretting that unpleasant little scene in the hall. He had only been trying to protect her, she knew, but she neither wanted nor needed his protection. Even so, she shouldn't have been so rotten to him…

Slanting her a sideways glance, Jared asked, 'Something wrong?'

Unwilling to cast a blight over things, she said, 'No. nothing…' Then, resting her head briefly on his shoulder, 'When we're going to spend a lovely long weekend together, what could be wrong?'

He smiled and reached to give her hand a squeeze.

Perdita found the journey—which put her in mind of the road movies she had seen—quite fascinating. The traffic was fairly heavy, forcing them to slow to a crawl as they passed towering hoardings and neon signs saying Eats or Burgers.

As the evening advanced, however, the traffic grew less and they started to make better time. Even so, it was getting dark and she was almost asleep before they began to drop down towards their destination.

'Look,' Jared said softly.

Opening her eyes, she caught her breath.

Ahead of them, spread like a many-jewelled cloak over the black floor of the desert, was Las Vegas, its glittering Strip setting the night sky ablaze with starbursts of brilliant light and colourful cascades of neon.

It was a sight she knew she would never forget, and she breathed, 'Isn't it romantic?'

'It certainly looks it from here,' Jared agreed, before adding a shade cynically, 'which only goes to prove the old saying, "distance lends enchantment".'

As they drove into town she could both see and hear that every hotel and casino was bursting with life and colour, movement and noise.

There were more than enough brilliant lights and flashing neon signs to turn night into day, and she could quite easily believe that this was a place that never slept.

Jared had chosen a hotel which proved to be relatively quiet and secluded, with only a small casino for the hotel guests and none of the ranks of slot machines which, he told her, most of the other hotels boasted.

When they had settled into their suite, Jared asked, 'Would you like to go downstairs to eat, and maybe later pay a visit to the casino?'

Having no inclination to do either, she answered, 'I don't really mind. Would *you* like to?'

He shook his head. 'I'd much prefer to eat up here, and, though I occasionally play roulette, I'm not much of a gambler.'

Finding they were in perfect accord, they shared a quiet supper in their suite before showering and going to bed.

After a wonderful night of tender and passionate love-making, they awoke early and had breakfast on their balcony, the better to enjoy the sunshine and the warm desert air.

Feeling carefree, on top of the world, Perdita stretched luxuriously and remarked, 'If this is the sort of "dangerous escapade" that Dad has always tried to warn me about, all I can say is, I wish I'd done it sooner.'

Intending it to be just a light-hearted remark she was surprised by Jared's reaction.

His face serious, he said, 'I have grave doubts about you doing it at all. I should never have persuaded you.'

'I didn't need much persuading,' she pointed out.

'Look, my love—' he took her hand and gripped it tightly '—this kind of hole and corner thing isn't really for us. Let's get married.'

'But we will as soon as Dad—'

'No, I mean now. Today. I want everyone to know you're my wife, not think you're just some bit of fluff who warms my bed.'

'Who cares what anyone else thinks?'

'I do.' Lifting her hand to his lips, he kissed the palm. 'Let's go and buy a ring and get married at one of the wedding chapels.'

As she started to shake her head, he said, 'It may seem a bit sleazy, but we'll have a proper wedding with a dress and all the trimmings as soon as your father's better.'

'No, it's not that…'

'What is it, then?'

'I would be quite happy to get married here, so long as we can keep it a secret for the time being.'

Seeing him frown, she added quickly, 'I can't chance Dad finding out until all these tests are over and done with and I know his heart is strong enough to stand the shock.'

'Suppose it never is?'

'It will be,' she said confidently.

They were married that afternoon in a quiet little chapel on the edge of town. The old adobe chapel was bare and white, with a few unpretentious flowers and a single mellow bell that rang joyously.

The simple ceremony was soon over and when she and

Jared walked out into the sunshine hand in hand they were man and wife.

'Now what would you like to do?' he asked.

Totally blissful and without a care in the world, she said, 'What I'd really like to do is see something of the desert.'

'Then we'll go for a nice long drive, and later this evening, if you'd like to, we'll have a celebratory meal at the Santecopa and stay for the cabaret and the dancing.'

'Sounds lovely,' she agreed happily.

After a lovely and memorable drive through the varied and rugged desert terrain, they returned to their hotel in Las Vegas to have a shower, before walking to the Santecopa, which was just around the corner.

Perdita, who had showered while Jared was confirming their table booking, had just finished dressing when the phone in their suite rang.

More than a little surprised, she picked it up and said, 'Hello?'

'Dita, I've been trying to get hold of you all afternoon.' Martin's voice was urgent. 'Your father's had another heart attack, and this time it may be touch and go.'

'Oh, dear God,' she breathed. Then, in a panic, 'What am I going to do?'

'Leave everything to me. I've just flown in and I'm downstairs in the lobby. I've got a cab waiting and two tickets on the next plane to Los Angeles if we can get to the airport in time.'

'I'll be down at once.'

Slamming the phone down, she rushed through to the bedroom where Jared was just emerging from the shower. 'Dad's had another heart attack,' she choked out fearfully.

Throwing aside the towel, he reached for his clothes. 'We'll fly straight to Los Angeles—'

'No, it would be best if you stayed here—'

Already pulling on his clothes, he said, 'Don't be foolish. I can't let you go alone.'

'Martin's going to take me,' she told him breathlessly. 'He's in the lobby now. He's got tickets on the next flight and a taxi waiting.'

Seizing her bag and a jacket, she ran, saying over her shoulder, 'As soon as I know how things are, I'll let you know.'

On her way down in the lift she happened to notice her rings and, taking them off, she slipped them into her locket and snapped it shut.

The flight to Los Angeles was a mercifully short one and they were soon descending through the evening smog. But the taxi drive to Mardale, fraught with anxiety as it was, seemed to take an age.

When they arrived at the large modern hospital, apart from the accident and emergency wing, it was relatively quiet and seemed on the point of settling down for the night.

An urgent enquiry at the main reception desk sent them hurrying up to the intensive care coronary unit, where they were stopped by a locked door with a keypad, a voice grille, and a closed-circuit television camera.

A disembodied male voice said, 'This is a limited entry unit, so please state your business.'

'I'm Miss Boyd.' Perdita kept her voice steady with an effort. 'I've come to see my father, John Boyd. Earlier today he suffered a heart attack and I understand he's dangerously ill.'

There was a long pause, then the voice said, 'We don't appear to have a patient of that name listed. If you'll wait a moment I'll try and get hold of the doctor in charge.'

After an agonizing wait, the door opened and a short balding man with cold blue eyes and an irascible manner appeared.

Closing the door behind him, he said brusquely, 'Miss

Boyd, I'm Dr Sondheim. You appear to have misunderstood or been misinformed—' his expression made it abundantly clear which he believed '—about the severity of your father's condition. Though he had what might loosely be described as a heart attack, it was an extremely mild one, and I can assure you that he's in no immediate danger.'

Perdita released the breath she'd been holding in a sob of relief as Martin asked, 'You're quite sure about that?'

The doctor gave him an exceedingly frosty look and said, 'Quite sure.'

'Please can we see him?' Perdita begged.

'This is the *intensive care* unit and your father is in the normal coronary unit.'

'Can we see him there?'

'My dear young lady, we can't possibly allow people to come and go at all hours disturbing our patients,' he said severely.

Then, as though to quash any possible argument, 'And the absolute rule is, no visitors at night unless the patient is very seriously ill, which happily your father is not.'

Taking pity on her, he added in a slightly softer tone, 'I strongly suggest that you go home and stop worrying. For the next twenty-four hours all your father needs is rest and quiet. When the twenty-four hours are up, we can resume the tests, and a couple of days after that you'll have him home, safe and sound.

'Now, if you'll excuse me, I have patients to attend to who *are* seriously ill.'

Before she could even thank him, he had keyed in a number and disappeared back inside, shutting the door firmly behind him and leaving them standing in the dimly lit, deserted corridor.

After all the previous worry, the sheer relief of finding her father was in no immediate danger had made Perdita start to tremble inwardly and turned her legs to water.

Watching her a shade anxiously, Martin asked, 'Are you happy to leave it at that?'

Where a more gentle approach might have left some doubts, Dr Sondheim's brusque, down-to-earth manner had effectively put her mind at rest and, pulling herself together, she nodded.

'Then we'd better find a hotel for the night.'

'No,' she said decidedly. 'I need to phone Jared and then get straight back to Las Vegas.'

She had half expected Martin to try and dissuade her from returning but, rather to her surprise, he accompanied her out of the hospital without a word.

When they got outside, with unsteady fingers she fumbled in her bag for her phone, only to find it wasn't there.

'Lend me your phone,' she said to Martin.

After feeling in his pocket, he said, 'Sorry, I don't seem to have it with me.'

'Then I'll just pop back into the hospital and find a pay phone.'

He caught her arm. 'Is there any point in phoning? After all, he's probably gone to bed by now. Wouldn't it make more sense to get the next plane back and surprise him?'

'You're right. But we'll need to phone for a taxi.'

As she spoke, headlights approached and a cab drew up a short distance away and dropped a young couple, who hurried straight into the hospital.

'We're in luck,' Martin exclaimed, signalling the driver, and a moment later they were in the cab and heading back to the airport. There was comparatively little traffic about and they made good time.

Perdita had expected Martin to go straight back to San Jose and was surprised when he asked for two tickets on the next flight to Vegas.

'There's really no need to come with me,' she protested.

But, a determined look on his fair face, he said, 'You've had one hell of a night, and there's no way I'm letting you go alone.'

Not content with accompanying her on the flight, he insisted on getting a cab and escorting her back to the hotel.

Apart from when they had made a quick visit to the airport restrooms to wash their hands and freshen up, he hadn't left her side for a moment.

She was well aware that, after the unkind way she had treated him, she should be grateful for all the care he had lavished on her but, even so, that amount of mollycoddling irritated her.

Although it was now the early hours of the morning, on reaching the floodlit Imperial Palace they found that the casino was still in full swing.

When, instead of just saying goodbye and leaving her there, Martin asked the taxi driver to wait and followed her into the lobby, her irritation overflowed. 'For heaven's sake, Martin, you don't need to take me right back to the suite.'

Looking hurt, he said, 'Earlier I noticed the hotel had an all night coffee bar, so I thought I'd snatch a quick cup before I started back.'

Feeling guilty at her own thoughtlessness, she said, 'Of course... I'm sorry.'

Then, sincerely, 'You've been absolutely great. I really can't thank you enough for all your help.'

'You know I'll always be here for you.'

Touched, she stood on tiptoe and kissed his cheek, promising, 'I'll give you a ring tomorrow,' before hurrying to the lift.

As the doors slid open she glanced back and caught a glimpse of Martin taking his cellphone from his pocket. So he *had* got it after all.

When the lift stopped at the seventh floor, she walked along the deserted corridor until she got to suite 704.

Earlier she had dropped one of the card keys they had been

given into her bag so, rather than wake Jared, she would go in quietly, slip into bed beside him and snuggle close.

With a little smile of anticipation, she pictured his surprise and pleasure when he awoke and realized she was back.

The card slid silently into the slot and the door opened with the slightest of clicks. She crossed the sitting room—which was in semi-darkness, the only light coming in from the flood-lighting outside—and opened the bedroom door.

A single bedside lamp was lit and in its soft glow she saw a man with dark hair who appeared to be sleeping and, standing beside the bed, a naked woman, her long red hair falling around smooth white shoulders and voluptuous breasts.

For the space of a heartbeat, Perdita thought she was in the wrong suite.

Then her eyes confirmed what her brain was refusing to accept. Though she had never set eyes on the woman before, the man was undoubtedly Jared.

As Perdita stood, shocked into immobility, the redhead began to pull on her clothes.

Jared had always had a thing about redheads. The thought fell like an ice crystal into Perdita's frozen mind. Then, like some zombie, she turned and walked away, out of the suite, out of Jared's life.

Her mind feeling jarred, incapable of coherent thought, she got into the lift and pressed the first floor button.

When she reached the lobby, almost as if he had been ex-pecting her, Martin appeared and walked towards her.

Dully, she said, 'I want to go home.'

He asked no questions, merely said, 'The cab's still waiting so let's go.'

During the dreadful days that followed, Martin was a tower of strength. He made no comment and asked no questions. He merely took care of her, encouraging her to sleep, stopping phone calls and visitors and reminding her to eat and drink.

Even through the thick haze of pain and misery that engulfed her, she recognized that he was doing everything in his power to please her and make her happy once more.

But the one thing he couldn't do, the one thing she desperately needed to do, was expunge from her memory the sight of a redheaded woman whose naked breasts were like alabaster...

A knock at the door brought her back to the present with a start and, shaken by the vividness of those memories, she paused to try and gather herself before calling, 'Come in.'

Hilary appeared with a small case and, catching sight of Perdita's face, queried, 'Is something wrong?'

'No, no... I was miles away.'

Proffering the case, Hilary said a shade doubtfully, 'I'm not sure whether this will be big enough. What do you think?'

'Oh, this should be fine, thanks,' Perdita told her.

When Hilary had gone, Perdita packed the case, finding it was quite adequate for the small amount she was taking, and put it ready to go in the car.

After a little thought, she changed into a simple oatmeal dress with a loose jacket and open-toed shoes and put a matching handbag by the case.

Then, with half an hour or so to spare, she returned to the sunny patio to keep Sam company and try to regain her equanimity.

Jared was back rather earlier than he had anticipated and, when their cases had been stowed in the boot, they set off, purring north-eastwards along the St Helena Highway.

'How far is it to Don and Estelle's?' she asked.

'About five miles along the Valley,' he told her. 'Their place is called Villa Rosa.'

Apart from that brief exchange, the short journey proved to be a silent one.

When they drew up outside the Villa Rosa, Perdita saw it was a sprawling one-storey white painted frame house, its porch engulfed in climbing roses which made the air heady with scent.

Jared led the way round the back where quite a number of people were already assembled by the poolside barbecue, drinks in their hands.

Two men were tending the massive barbecue, one of them bare-chested and wearing frayed cut-offs and flip-flops, the other sporting a chef's hat and apron.

There was an atmosphere of informal friendliness that was relaxed and pleasant. Most of the women wore cotton trousers and tops, the men shorts and T-shirts. Against the somewhat unprepossessing display of knees and paunches, Jared looked coolly elegant.

All the guests, men and women alike, had what Perdita was starting to recognize as an authentic West Coast tan.

A tall, nice-looking woman with soft dark hair and big brown eyes detached herself from the crowd and came to greet them, smiling from one to the other.

'Jared...' She gave him a hug. Then, holding out her hand, 'And you must be Perdita. How nice to meet you. I'm so glad you could come.

'I'm Estelle...' Patting her sizable bulge, she added, 'And this is Don Junior. An active lad who will almost certainly grow up to be a footballer.'

As Perdita smiled, Don came over to hand them each a glass of white wine and add his greetings to those of his wife.

'By the way,' he went on, turning to Jared, 'Greg's here. He was just telling me about a new grape variety he's thinking of planting...'

As the two men fell into conversation, with a fondly exasperated glance at her husband, Estelle said to Perdita, 'Don never talks about anything but wine if there's anyone there willing to listen.'

Then, linking her arm through Perdita's, 'Come and say hello to some of our mutual neighbours.'

For a while they moved from group to group, meeting people and chatting. Everyone was pleasant and friendly, and *curious*.

Understandably so, as almost everyone seemed to have assumed that Jared was a bachelor. Now to find he had a wife, and a wife with an English accent, caused a minor sensation.

Most of the women asked, 'Have you been married very long?'

Most of the men, 'Where has Jared been hiding you?'

Having had no guidance from Jared, and with no idea how to answer their questions, Perdita said vaguely that they had been married for quite a while, adding that she had been living and working in London.

When she failed to elaborate, it was plain that a few of them would have liked to have questioned her further, but good manners prevailed and the talk moved on to a variety of other things.

She was discussing Valley life with Joanie and Howard who, she soon discovered, lived next door to Wolf Rock, when Estelle excused herself and went to find Don and chivy him into replenishing the dwindling stock of chilled white wine.

After a while the conversation was interrupted by a man in a chef's hat calling, 'Food's up, folks... Come and grab a plate while it's hot.'

With cheerful efficiency, Perdita's glass was refilled and she was handed a plate containing a variety of barbecued meat and salad and some cutlery rolled in a napkin.

Moving out of the crowd, she sat down at a small umbrella-shaded table a little apart from the rest.

There had been no sign of Jared since they had left him talking to Don, but now she noticed him sitting on a swing-seat with a predatory-looking blonde.

The woman, who must have been in her late twenties or early thirties, was undeniably beautiful beneath the heavy make-up.

She was wearing a skimpy top and the briefest of shorts that would have looked more in keeping on a teenager, and was leaning towards Jared, all fluttering eyelashes and pliant golden curves.

Her breast was pressed against his upper arm and one hand was spread, open-fingered, across his shirt front. When she said something, obviously teasing, his white smile flashed in response.

'May I join you?' Estelle appeared by Perdita's side, plate in hand.

'Of course.' Looking up at the other woman, Perdita managed a smile.

As Estelle began to tuck into a large steak, Perdita's eyes were drawn once more to the pair on the swing-seat. As she watched, the blonde's red-tipped fingers unfastened a couple of buttons and slipped inside Jared's shirt.

He caught her hand and withdrew it but, instead of just letting it go, he held it.

Watching those glistening red lips pouting at him seductively, Perdita felt a fierce pang of jealousy and anger. How *could* he bring her here and then leave her to her own devices while he flirted openly with another woman?

'I can tell what you're thinking,' Estelle remarked suddenly. 'But don't let Marcia's antics bother you. Even though she's got a perfectly good husband of her own, she's never been able to resist trying her wiles on every man who comes within range.

'Since she reached the ripe old age of thirty, she's been even worse. It's as if she's terrified of losing her sex appeal.'

Receiving no immediate response, Estelle went on, 'You can see it's not Jared's fault. He's doing absolutely nothing to encourage her.'

'Unless you count holding her hand,' Perdita said tightly.

Estelle shook her head. 'If you look more closely, I think you'll find that *she's* holding *his* hand. All Jared's doing is trying, as gracefully as possible, to fend her off.'

When Perdita turned bleak eyes on her, the other woman went on gently, 'I can see you're head over heels in love with him and, believe me, I know only too well what it's like to be jealous.

'When Don and I were first married, if he so much as looked at another woman I used to fly into a jealous rage. He wanted me to trust him, but somehow, even though he swore he loved me, I couldn't. That lack of trust and my unreasonable jealousy almost broke up our marriage. It's only by the grace of God that I woke up in time and realized that if I didn't change, I'd lose him...'

As Perdita listened, she glanced at the swing-seat once more. Jared had vanished and the blonde was sitting there alone, nursing an untouched plate of food and looking disconsolate.

'Now our marriage is as firm as a rock,' Estelle went on. 'I trust him implicitly and I make sure he knows it...'

'But, in your case, I'm sure Don's worthy of your trust. Not all men are.'

'That's quite true.'

'So is there any way to tell the difference?'

'I think so. If you can put jealousy to one side and start to think clearly about what kind of man you've got, you'll soon know.

'Is he basically a one woman man? Is he willing to be faithful? Is he *capable* of being faithful? Has he enough moral fibre? Enough self-control?

'If the answer to those questions is yes, he should be worthy of any woman's trust.'

Then, a shade hesitantly, 'I don't know what's wrong between you and Jared, and I don't want to know. But I'll tell you one thing—though I've seen plenty of women vying for his attention, I've never seen him show the slightest interest in any of them.

'So much so that if he hadn't been quite obviously straight I might well have thought—' She stopped speaking abruptly.

Then, after a moment, sounding embarrassed, uncomfortable, she said, 'I'm sorry. I should learn to keep my big mouth shut. I can only apologize if I've offended you by sticking my nose into your affairs.

'But I very much hope that you and I can be friends. I like and respect Jared, so when I see two nice people who obviously love each other having problems, it seems a shame to—'

Coming to life, Perdita broke in quickly, 'You haven't offended me. In fact I'm really grateful for such plain speaking.'

Then, feeling a sudden urge to confide in this friendly, sensible woman, she admitted, 'And you're quite right about me being jealous. I never could help it. So many women seemed to find Jared irresistible that he could have had his pick—'

'Presumably he did. He picked you.'

'And that should have been enough?'

'It wasn't?'

'At first it was, but I suppose I've always been afraid that I wasn't beautiful enough, clever enough or interesting enough to hold him.'

'But when it's obvious how much he loves you…'

'The truth is, he *doesn't* love me,' Perdita told her flatly.

'You're joking, of course!' Estelle exclaimed. 'Earlier, while you were talking to Joanie and Howie, I was watching him watching you and I'd stake my life that he's mad about you.'

Just as she finished speaking, Don called, 'Estelle, can

you spare a minute? I can't find the cheesecakes you were talking about earlier.'

'They're in the fridge,' she answered. Then, rising to her feet, 'Don't worry, I've finished eating. I'll come and get them.'

Edging round the table, she said to Perdita, 'Men! Bless their little hearts. As far as they're concerned, fridges are only used to keep wine and beer cold.' Patting her bulge fondly, she added, 'I expect this one will be just the same.'

Estelle had been right about one thing at least, Perdita thought as she watched the other woman walk away. She *did* love Jared. Though, until then, she had refused to acknowledge it, even to herself, she had never stopped loving him.

Was it remotely possible that, in spite of his denial, he still loved her?

She felt a faint stirring of hope.

If by any chance he did, and that love had survived all her mistrust and jealousy, then it must have been strong and enduring indeed.

But if he *had* loved her like that, surely he wouldn't have taken another woman to bed on what should have been their wedding night?

Yet she had seen it with her own eyes.

So how could she believe he loved her? How could she trust him?

Common sense told her she couldn't.

But what if, in this case, common sense was wrong?

She was still turning it over in her mind when Jared appeared and strolled towards her.

Taking a seat opposite, he said, 'I'm sorry if I appeared to abandon you but I was…held up.'

'I noticed,' she said tartly, then bit her lip in vexation. Why on earth had she admitted that she had been watching him?

His dark head tilted a little to one side, he studied her before saying mockingly, 'Anyone would think you were jealous.'

'Not at all,' she assured him coolly.

'I take it you've been meeting people?'

'Yes, but it was a bit awkward.'

He raised a dark brow. 'They weren't friendly?'

'Extremely friendly. They were also curious as to how long we'd been married and where I'd suddenly sprung from.'

'What did you tell them?'

'That we'd been married for some time, but that I'd been living and working in England.'

'Very diplomatic.'

Glancing at her barely touched plate, he went on, 'When you've finished eating, I thought we might make a move.'

'I really don't want any more. Have you...?'

He shook his head. 'I wasn't hungry either.'

Taking a deep breath, she asked, 'Jared, do we *have* to go to Las Vegas?'

'Yes, we do,' he said quietly. 'It's high time this whole thing was brought out into the open before it's buried once and for all.'

Rising, he took her hand and pulled her to her feet. Then, still hand in hand, they went to say their thanks and goodbyes to Estelle and Don.

'Going so soon?' Don asked.

'We're off to Vegas for a couple of days,' Jared said lightly.

Noting their clasped hands, Estelle smiled. 'Well, Don Junior's piggy bank is empty and he still needs a baby buggy. So, if you happen to play roulette, put ten dollars on zero for me.'

'Why zero?' Perdita asked.

'When Don and I first got together we had a cat we called Zero, and he brought us luck.'

CHAPTER TEN

THE journey was a long one and, while they travelled, Perdita found herself going over and over in her mind what Estelle had said.

'If you can put jealousy to one side and start to think clearly about what kind of man you've got, you'll soon know.

'Is he basically a one woman man? Is he willing to be faithful? Is he *capable* of being faithful? Has he enough moral fibre? Enough self-control?"

Everything she had ever learned about Jared made her answer *yes* to all those questions.

So why had she doubted him? Admittedly, what she'd seen had looked pretty damning, but why hadn't she at least *listened* to him?

Thinking back, she remembered how he'd said, "There might be another explanation, rather than the obvious?"

In truth, it had all seemed so cut and dried that she hadn't. But suppose there was? Suppose her own jealousy had prevented her looking for it?

For the first time real doubts began to take root and grow with staggering rapidity.

During the early part of their relationship she had been naive and inexperienced and madly in love with him. Had he wanted to, he could have seduced her with ease, and he must have been well aware of that.

But he hadn't. He had shown endless patience. *She* had been the one to make the first move.

And when he had told her that he'd been celibate since she had left him, she had believed him implicitly.

So why, in those circumstances, would a man who could exert such amazing self-control stoop to entertaining another woman on his wedding night?

Looked at in that light, it didn't make sense.

Those new, revolutionary thoughts were still going through her mind when they crossed the State border into Nevada.

By the time they approached Las Vegas, night had descended with the suddenness it always did in desert regions.

Though on this occasion Perdita knew what to expect, she still caught her breath at the first sight of the brilliant, many-faceted cluster of lights that lay in the surrounding blackness like a bejewelled brooch.

Jared had been quiet and withdrawn during the latter part of the journey, as if he were thinking something serious through. Now, a strange note in his voice, he asked, 'Still think it's romantic?'

Unsure of his mood, or exactly what he was getting at, she decided to play safe. 'I think it's still got the Wow! factor.'

'Nicely put,' he commented a shade mockingly, before falling silent again.

As they drove into Las Vegas itself, she asked, 'Where exactly are we staying?'

'I'll give you one guess.'

Of course. She'd been a fool to ask.

Wondering exactly what he had in mind, she queried, 'Did you manage to get the same suite?'

'As a matter of fact, I did.'

Feeling uneasy, she asked no further questions, but while

Jared picked his way through the brightly lit streets she watched his face.

He appeared to be still mulling something over, something grave and important, judging by his sombre expression.

Only when they reached the Imperial Palace did he snap out of it, his earlier look of troubled irresolution gone. Now he looked stern and resolved, like a man who had made a bleak but necessary decision.

Leaving the car in the underground parking lot, they went through to the lobby to check in.

The man at the reception desk greeted Jared cheerfully. 'Nice to see you again, Mr Dangerfield.'

'Nice to see you, Patrick. How are things?'

'Sure they're not bad at all.' Then, with a glance at Perdita, 'You're not here alone this time.'

'No, I thought I'd bring my wife.'

Patrick beamed at them both. 'Good to have you here, Mrs Dangerfield. I hope you enjoy your visit.'

Perdita thanked him and returned his smile.

Checking in completed, they took the lift up to the seventh floor, one of the bell hops following with their small amount of luggage.

When Jared opened the door to suite 704, Perdita forced her reluctant legs to carry her inside.

The decor appeared to be unchanged and a glimpse of the bed, with its pink sheets and pink-frilled pillowcases, brought back all the memories she'd been trying for three years to leave behind.

But, as she faced them squarely with her new-found knowledge of herself and Jared, they became relatively unimportant, no longer able to hurt.

When the bell hop had departed, pocketing a generous tip, Jared said, 'We've a table booked for dinner, but I thought perhaps we might pay a visit to the casino first?'

Perdita was no particular fan of gambling but, still unsure how to say what she now knew she wanted to say, she answered, 'Yes, that would be nice.'

'Then if you'd like to go ahead and get changed, I've a phone call to make.'

When she had freshened up in the pink-tiled bathroom, she swirled her hair into an elegant chignon and made-up lightly, before putting on her cocktail dress and sandals. A touch of perfume and a pair of glittering drop earrings fastened to her small lobes added the finishing touch.

She had just finished when Jared appeared and, with barely a glance, disappeared into the bathroom.

Only too conscious of the fact that he seemed to be deliberately avoiding her, she went through to the sitting room with a heavy heart.

As soon as he returned, freshly shaved and looking coolly elegant in a well-cut dinner jacket and black tie, they made their way down to the casino.

At the entrance desk, Jared paused to exchange a wad of dollars for a pile of fat pink plastic one hundred dollar chips.

Left to her own devices for a moment, Perdita glanced around. The big room with its brightly lit tables, each manned by a croupier, was windowless and, suspended in a kind of timeless oblivion, it could easily have been any hour of the day or night.

Glamorous hostesses, distinguished by black dresses and small rhinestone tiaras, took care of any single male guests, while long-legged waitresses, seemingly clad in little but pink feathers, went to and fro carrying trays of drinks and snacks.

Most of the people there were wearing evening dress and an unmistakable aura of affluence. The air was full of the smell of wine and expensive perfume and noisy with the popping of champagne corks, the calls of the croupiers and the rattle of roulette wheels.

Returning to her side, Jared asked, 'What do you fancy playing?'

'I...I don't really know... Nothing too complicated. I've never played before.'

'Then I suggest you try your hand at roulette.' He steered her to the nearest table with an empty chair and, having settled her into her seat, put the pile of chips in front of her.

The croupier, who wore a badge inscribed 'Marylou', smiled at them and said a nasal, 'Welcome.'

No one else at the table looked up, but almost immediately a waitress appeared by their side and asked, 'What can I get you?'

Though Jared looked in anything but a celebratory mood, he ordered champagne.

Marylou droned, 'Place your bets.'

Following the lead of the player next to her, Perdita slid one of her chips onto a red numbered square and watched the hypnotic blur of the wheel as it spun.

The ball clicked into a space and, after calling out the winning colour and number, Marylou raked in the chips.

Perdita soon discovered that while everyone else seemed riveted, she found roulette repetitive and worrying rather than exciting.

Unwilling to lose Jared's money, she played cautiously but, even so, the pile of chips was disappearing with great rapidity.

When he suggested getting more, she shook her head.

She was down to the last three when she suddenly recalled Estelle saying, 'Don Junior's piggy bank is empty and he still needs a baby buggy, so if you play roulette, put ten dollars on zero for me.'

With a surge of recklessness, probably engendered by two glasses of champagne, she pushed her remaining three chips onto the relevant square.

The number came up.

Collecting her winning chips, she had started to rise when

Jared, who had been standing behind her, pressed her back into her seat.

'I really don't want to lose this,' she protested. 'It's your money and—'

'No, it's *your* money.'

'Then I want it for Don Junior's piggy bank.'

'That's fine by me but, now your luck's turned, you should give it at least one more try.'

'The same number?' she asked.

'Why not? It's got as much chance of coming up as any of the others.'

She was wondering how much to risk when Jared murmured, 'Go for it,' and, leaning forward, pushed the entire pile back on to zero.

While she held her breath, the ball rattled round the wheel and once again settled with a click into the same slot.

A sound like a sigh went round the table as Marylou, her face impassive, raked in the losing chips and paid the winner.

When Jared had converted the chips back into cash, he presented Perdita with a thick wad of notes.

She shook her head. 'I'd much rather you took care of it.'

'OK.' He thrust it into his pocket. 'When we get back you can put it in Don Junior's piggy bank. Now, about ready to eat?'

She still didn't feel particularly hungry but, reluctant to return to their suite with Jared in his present mood, she agreed, 'Yes, if you are.'

The spectacular dining room, its crystal chandeliers glittering like diamonds, was horseshoe-shaped with a central dance floor from which the tables radiated like the spokes of a wheel.

On a raised dais at the back, where later there would be a cabaret act, a small orchestra was playing dance music and a number of couples were circling the floor.

All the tables appeared to be full, but after Jared had murmured something to the maître d' they were shown to a table on the edge of the dance floor where a bottle of champagne was waiting in an ice bucket.

Perdita noticed that there were three chairs and three champagne glasses.

A moment later the orchestra began a romantic slow foxtrot and, rising, Jared held out his hand to her and asked, 'Would you like to dance?'

She could see at once that his mood had changed, that he had, temporarily at least, thrown off the devil that had been riding him.

They hadn't danced together since her eighteenth birthday party and, recalling how happy they had been that night, Perdita felt as if a giant fist had closed around her heart. Would they ever be quite so happy again?

She got to her feet a shade unsteadily.

Jared, who moved with a wholly masculine grace, was a good dancer and easy to follow, and she fitted into his arms as if she belonged there.

After a few moments he bent his dark head and they danced cheek to cheek, as they had that last time.

His jaw was smooth and she could smell the faint yet lingering scent of his aftershave.

Letting go of all the worries and uncertainty, Perdita closed her eyes and, the music filling her mind, let herself drift.

After a couple of dreamy foxtrots there was an intermission, and she was still suspended in a bubble of happiness when, an arm at her waist, Jared led her back to their table.

As he seated her, looking at the empty chair and the extra wine glass, Perdita remarked, 'It looks as if you were expecting someone to join us.'

'I was, originally. In fact that was the whole purpose of the visit. But then I had second thoughts and asked her not to come,' he ended with finality.

But, curious, Perdita decided to pursue it. As lightly as possible, she asked, 'So who is this mystery woman?'

After the slightest hesitation, he told her, 'A lady by the name of Linda. She used to be a hostess here, but now she's married to the casino manager.'

With a sudden flash of insight, Perdita said, 'And she was the woman I saw in your bedroom.'

It was a statement, not a question, but he answered evenly, 'That's right.'

Taking a deep breath, she began, 'Jared, there's something I want to tell you—'

'What the hell's going on?' A man's furious voice cut across her words.

She looked up to see Martin hovering threateningly, his face an unbecoming brick-red.

'Unless you want to get thrown out, I suggest you sit down and lower your voice,' Jared said coldly.

'I'm not here to take orders from you. I'm here to fetch my fiancée.' Grasping Perdita's wrist, he tried to pull her to her feet.

'Leave her alone!' Jared said quietly and, a white line around his mouth, he half rose.

Recovering a little from the shock of the other man's sudden appearance, and seeing the maître'd looking in their direction, Perdita said urgently, 'Please, Martin, sit down and let's talk.'

After a moment Jared resumed his seat and Martin sat down in the spare chair, one man quietly watchful, the other openly belligerent.

Turning to Martin, Perdita asked, 'How did you know where to find me?'

'I felt sure something was wrong, so I did a bit of digging. When I discovered that Dangerfield had recently bought Salingers, and that the phone calls I was making to New York were being put through to his place in California, I got on the next plane.

'The housekeeper told me where you'd gone.'

His voice full of rage and frustration, he demanded, 'How the devil could you let yourself fall for his tricks a second time?'

'I'm sorry, I know I owe you an explanation—'

'Damn right you do! I want to know what the hell you're doing here with him when you'll be marrying me in a few weeks.'

Obviously resenting the other man's bullying tactics, Jared was about to step in when, meeting his eyes, Perdita begged, 'Please, Jared, will you leave this to me?'

'If that's what you want.'

'It is.'

Turning to Martin, she went on, 'The thing is, I won't be marrying you.'

Before he could protest, she added quickly, 'Three years ago when you came here to fetch me after Dad had his heart attack, Jared and I were already man and wife. We'd been married that day.

'But you knew that, didn't you?'

Looking uncomfortable, he said, 'Not at the time. I only found out later. But surely your marriage was annulled.'

She shook her head. 'I thought it was. I thought I was free to marry you. But, when I met Jared again, I found we were still married. I should have told you straight away, I know, but...'

'Instead, you let yourself get embroiled for a second time.' He shot Jared a malevolent look. 'Well, now *I'll* make sure it's annulled.'

'It's too late for an annulment.'

His face growing even redder, Martin snarled, 'So, having kept me at arms' length for almost three years, you've been fool enough to sleep with him! Or did he force you?'

'No, he didn't force me.'

Looking unconvinced, Martin said, 'Then we'll just have to postpone the wedding until your divorce comes through.'

'I'm sorry, Martin, but I don't want to marry you. I should never have said yes in the first place.'

'You've let that swine influence you,' he said furiously. 'And you know as well as I do that you can't trust him.'

'But I *do* trust him,' she said clearly.

Conscious that Jared was sitting stock-still, she added, 'He told me he hadn't so much as looked at another woman that night and I believe him. I should have realized sooner that he was telling the truth.'

'You must be mad!' Martin burst out. 'You *saw* another woman in his bedroom.'

'How do you know what I saw? I never told you.'

He looked momentarily put out, then he rallied. 'But you *did*, didn't you?'

'It's quite possible that it was just a mistake, that she got into the wrong suite.'

'You'd be an idiot if you believed that.'

'I *do* believe it.'

'Can you also believe that she not only got into the wrong suite, but into the wrong bed with a strange man?' he jeered.

'She wasn't in bed.'

As though making up his mind, Martin pulled an envelope from his pocket. 'It's a good thing I had the foresight to bring these. Take a look at them and tell me if you still think it was just a mistake.'

In the envelope were several photographs of the redhead and Jared in bed together. Though they weren't actually touching, they were lying close, the covers pushed down so she could see they were naked. Both appeared to be asleep.

Just for an instant Perdita's faith was shaken.

Seeing it in her face, Martin said triumphantly, 'Pretty damning, wouldn't you say?'

'Where did you get these?' she asked quietly.

'It doesn't matter where I got them.'

'But it does,' she insisted. 'They could be fakes. It's amazing what can be done these days with—'

'Of course they're not fakes,' he snarled.

A growing suspicion made her push it. 'How can you be so sure?'

After a moment Martin admitted boldly, 'Because I arranged to have them taken.'

'*You* arranged to have them taken...? Why?'

'Because I guessed what would happen as soon as your back was turned—'

Her suspicion confirmed, she said, 'You mean you set him up.'

She saw guilt written all over his face before he protested, 'How can you believe I'd do such a thing? You know perfectly well I—'

She cut short his blustering. 'Well, it should be easy to prove. As you may have noticed, because you're sitting in it, there was an extra chair and also a glass...'

When he looked blank, she added sweetly, 'Linda will be joining us shortly. She's agreed to tell me exactly what happened. So, if you don't want to be totally humiliated, I suggest you leave.'

'But Dita, I—'

'I'll let you have your ring back. In the meantime you'd better try and make your peace with Dad because I intend to tell him everything.'

Without another word Martin got to his feet and, looking like a man who had suffered a knockout blow, shambled away, leaving Perdita limp with reaction.

Jared, who had sat like a statue, his eyes fixed on her face, came to life and signalled a waiter, who opened and poured the champagne before producing leather-covered menus.

Seeing Perdita was in no state to choose, Jared ordered for them both.

When the waiter had gone, she found her voice and asked, 'Jared, why didn't you tell me all this five days ago?'

Turning those cool silvery eyes on her, he said flatly, 'I wasn't sure you'd believe me.'

'So that's why you brought me here... But, in that case, why did you change your mind and stop Linda coming?'

'Because of what I *thought* we meant to each other, I wanted you to *trust* me, to *believe* in me, to *know* me, to take my word without me having to prove it, and I finally realized that if you *couldn't* then it was no use.'

Though he spoke quietly there was so much passion in his voice that she felt scourged.

As he finished speaking, their first course arrived. Head down, she ate automatically without tasting a thing and with no real idea of what was on her plate.

They had reached the coffee stage before she was able to struggle free from the morass of conflicting emotions that had engulfed her.

Lifting her head, she looked up, her beautiful turquoise eyes brimming with tears, and said simply, 'Oh, Jared...'

He reached across the table and covered her hand with his. 'I'm sorry. Knowing Judson's part in it must have come as a shock to you.'

'I'm *glad* I know,' she said fiercely. 'You were right when you said he was cunning and deceitful and a liar. You should have added *ruthless*.

'He must have *caused* Dad's heart attack by telling him we were in Las Vegas together. He *wanted* it to happen so he had an excuse to get me away. How *could* he? The shock might have been fatal.'

'But it wasn't,' Jared pointed out. 'Luckily, your father's heart was strong enough to stand it.'

The slim hand resting on the white tablecloth clenched into a fist. 'But it might not have been.'

Taking her hand, Jared straightened her fingers one at a time, kissing each one as he did so.

'Bear in mind that he was mad about you, and jealousy is a cruel goad.'

'How *can* you be so magnanimous after everything he did to you?'

'I admit I haven't always felt that way. When I first found out what he'd done I could have cheerfully broken his neck.'

'I just *wish*…' She broke off, momentarily choked by tears. Then after a moment she went on, 'At the very least I should have *listened* to you. Given you the benefit of the doubt. If I hadn't been so bitterly jealous…'

He shook his head. 'I've come to realize it was asking a lot to expect you to give me the benefit of the doubt when at first even *I* wasn't sure what was going on.'

'Tell me what happened,' she said huskily.

A spasm of emotion crossed his face, but his voice was level as he began. 'After you'd gone, to pass the time I went down to the casino. I had a couple of drinks and played roulette until about twelve-thirty. Then, because I hadn't heard from you, I went to bed.

'I awoke in the early hours of the morning, muddled and with a thick head—later I learnt my drinks had been spiked— to find a strange woman in the bedroom getting dressed.

'At that moment I was certain of only two things. I'd never seen her before in my life, and I'd gone to bed alone. When I asked her what she was doing there, she swore she'd come into the wrong suite by mistake. She said that, as all the suites looked alike, she hadn't realized until she was about to get into bed. Adding that she was sorry she'd disturbed me, she headed for the door.

'By this time I was wide awake and feeling uneasy because I hadn't heard from you. In need of a cup of black coffee, I pulled on some clothes and took the elevator down.

'The night security guard was in the lobby and, when he spotted me, he remarked, "I'm afraid you've missed her".

'I must have looked blank because he said, "The young blonde girl you were with earlier yesterday evening. She's just this minute gone".

'I told him that he must be mistaken. But he insisted that he'd seen you and a tall fair man come in a short while before, and that while the man had hung around down here, you'd taken the elevator up. He added that you came down again after only a few minutes, and left with that same man.

'I know these security guards are trained to notice things and not make mistakes, and I began to wonder if he could be right.

'Suppose you *had* gone up to our suite and seen another woman leaving?

'I asked him if by any chance he'd seen anything of a striking redhead.

'He immediately said, "Oh, yes. Linda Dow… She came through here a little while ago. She's a hostess in the casino. If you're looking for her, at this time in the morning she'll no doubt be having a quiet drink in the room behind the bar.

'I thanked him and went in search of Miss Dow. She was where he'd said she'd be, and she didn't look too pleased to see me.

'However, she stuck to her story that she'd got into the wrong suite by mistake, and claimed she'd been looking for a somewhat drunken client who earlier that evening had hired her services.

'When I pressed her, she admitted that while she was in my bedroom a blonde had come in and gone straight out again without a word.

'I set off at once for the airport, but could find no sign of you. I wasn't sure whether you would have gone home or back to Los Angeles. As soon as it was a reasonable time, I phoned the hospital. I learnt that after a mild heart attack your father was doing well. But no one seemed to have seen anything of you.'

His voice holding an edge of strain now, he went on, 'After phoning several times, with still no sighting of you, I flew back to San Jose.

'When I got to Judson's house it appeared to be shut up. There was no sign of life. No one answered either the doorbell or the phone.

'The next day I went to JB's offices but was told that, apart from the ordinary office staff, everyone was away. No one seemed to know where.

'By this time I was fairly certain that you must be in Los Angeles so I flew there and for the best part of three days I hung around the hospital, hoping against hope to see you.

'At the same time I kept phoning Judson's house, without success. When I did finally manage to get through, it was Elmer Judson who answered.

'As soon as he realized who it was, he hung up.

'Then I learnt that your father's tests had been completed and he was to be discharged the next day. I felt sure he would be going to wherever you were, so I followed him back to San Jose and to Judson's house. Guessing what would happen if I rang the bell, I simply walked in.'

His voice harsh, he added, 'The rest you know.'

With a shiver, she said, 'I've never understood why you didn't fight back.'

'Because your father was still recovering from a heart attack I didn't want to make matters worse. I was hoping, if possible, to keep things low-key.'

Remembering his cut lip and the trickle of bright blood that had run down his chin, her voice full of pain, she insisted, 'You didn't have to let them beat you up. You could have stopped them.'

'Only by using my fists.'

Her face contorted, she said, 'Whereas I could have stopped them by saying just a couple of words.'

'Had you chosen to.'

'With that scene in the bedroom still so clear in my mind I didn't want to have to admit that we were married, admit what a fool I'd been.'

'I quite understand,' he said heavily. 'I'm not blaming you.'

But how many times had she blamed herself?

Unsteadily, she asked, 'How long were you in hospital?'

'Five days.'

'Five days!'

'The forced inactivity gave me time to think, and the conviction began to grow on me that I'd been deliberately set up. But you refused to see me or listen to me and, in any case, I had no proof. Then you delivered the coup de grâce by telling me you wanted an annulment. In desperation, I went back to Vegas to try and find out the truth.

'I eventually succeeded. Linda admitted that Judson had offered her five thousand dollars to do exactly as he said. He wanted you to see her in bed with me but, in case that didn't come off, he hired her boyfriend to take those pictures. When I asked her how they got into the suite, she admitted that one of the chambermaids, who was a friend of hers, had lent her a master key.

'Now I knew what I needed to know, but by the time I got back to San Jose you'd vanished.

'Elmer Judson was my only hope but, even when I told him we were married, he refused point-blank to help. He said you were better off without me, and advised me to get the marriage annulled.

'When, seeing nothing else for it, I told him how Martin had set me up, I could see by his expression that he already knew and approved.

'That was when I tumbled to the fact that I was fighting a losing battle. He and his son were in it together. The only one of the men who didn't know the truth was your father.

'During the days that followed I was sunk in black despair.

My company was almost on the rocks, but when I should have been working out some kind of rescue package, all I could think of was finding you.

'In the end it was my godfather who saved me, and I don't mean just financially. He said, "I know the future looks bleak right now, but concentrate on getting back in a position of strength. Then, if you still want her, I'm sure you can find her again."'

He stopped speaking and for the first time she became aware of the music and the voices, the laughter and the popping of champagne corks.

The orchestra came to the end of a medley and a minute or so later it was announced that the cabaret would begin shortly.

'Do you want to stay for the cabaret?' Jared asked.

With her heart and her mind so full, and so much that still needed to be said, Perdita shook her head.

A hand at her waist, he escorted her out of the restaurant and up to their suite.

She had hoped that once the door had closed behind them he might take her in his arms. But instead he asked politely, 'Perhaps you'd care to shower first?'

In silence she found her sponge bag and night things and went to clean her teeth and prepare for bed.

When she emerged, cool and scented and wearing an ivory satin nightdress and negligée, with scarcely a glance, Jared went into the bathroom and closed the door behind him.

Her heart sinking, she went into the living room and sat down on the couch.

When Jared came out of the bathroom, his hair still damp and wearing a short navy-blue silk robe, he looked surprised to see her still up.

'Not in bed yet? I thought you'd be tired.'

He looked tired, she thought with concern, drained, as if all the raw emotion of the evening had finally taken its toll, and she longed to tell him how much she loved him, longed to cradle his dark head against her breast.

'I am tired,' she admitted, 'but I've got too much going on in my mind to sleep.'

'In that case it might be as well to say what has to be said.' He let out his breath in a sigh before going on, 'I was wrong to try and force you to come back to me, and I can only ask your forgiveness for everything I put you through when I realized how very unwilling you were.

'If, when you've had a chance to think it over, you find you still love Judson, I'll give you a quick divorce. You may have to postpone your wedding for a while but I'll make it as speedy as possible.'

He sounded as if he couldn't wait to get rid of her, she thought unhappily.

Pride made her lift her chin. 'Very well. Though, even if you no longer want me, there's no way I'd marry Martin.'

'You've stopped loving him?'

'I've stopped *liking* him, which is even more important. I never did love him. I was fond of him, grateful for what he'd done for me...

'*Grateful*!' Her voice broke. 'He was quite prepared to wreck both our futures and to risk Dad's life to try and ensure his own happiness. And even when he knew we were married he never showed the slightest sign of remorse.'

'What made you so sure he knew?'

'I remembered that one day when he'd been talking to Elmer, he came off the phone looking badly shaken. Later, when we were alone, he said, "Even if you'd been foolish enough to marry Dangerfield, it would be easy to go to a lawyer and get an annulment".

'Though I didn't say anything, he must have seen how very unhappy I was, how hurt and bitterly disillusioned, but he didn't care a jot...'

Hearing the quiver in her voice, Jared said quietly, 'It's all over and done with. Time to bury the past and concentrate on the future.

'Tomorrow you can ring your father. Tell him that everything's settled. Salingers have agreed to buy fifty per cent of the shares and as soon as they have his formal acceptance they'll put into place the promised rescue package.

'You can add that you should be back in England some time next week. You needn't mention my name.'

She shook her head. 'I'm going to tell Dad the whole story.'

Looking startled, Jared said, 'You really intend to tell him everything?'

'Yes. It's time he knew exactly what Martin and Elmer are capable of.'

'Are you sure that's wise?'

'I'm sure it's *necessary*. It wouldn't be fair to you if I didn't.'

'As Judson's living in your father's house, it might make things difficult for you.'

'I have every intention of moving out. I'm going to cut free, find another job and a flat of my own. I'm sure Sally will look after Dad...'

It had been a long stressful day and, tiredness suddenly washing over her, she rubbed a hand across her eyes.

'You look ready for bed,' Jared remarked.

Rising to her feet, she agreed, 'I am now.'

When he made no move to accompany her, she asked, 'What about you?'

'I'll be sleeping on the couch.'

Her heart lurched drunkenly. 'Why?'

'I'm only human. If I sleep in the same bed I may not be able to keep my hands off you.'

'What if I said I don't want you to?'

'That's very tempting, but when love dies it's time to let go.'

In a small voice, she began, 'I know you don't love me, but I...'

'How do you know?'

'You've just said, "when love dies"...'

'I didn't mean *my* love.'

'But days ago you told me you no longer loved me. You said all that was left was lust.'

'I wish that was the truth; it would be easier to cope with.'

Hope suddenly filling her heart, she demanded, 'If it isn't, why did you say it?'

'It's hard to admit you still love someone who no longer loves you.'

'But I *do*! Love you, I mean. I've never stopped loving you.'

'I would like to believe that, but I can't. I think you're just trying to put right what you now see as an injustice.'

Without a word, she went into the bedroom and, fishing in her jewellery box, took out the gold locket that held her rings.

When she returned to the other room, Jared was sitting quite still, his head in his hands. When he dropped his hands and looked up, she held out the locket. 'If you don't believe I still love you, explain why I've kept these.'

Like a man in a dream he took it and, having used his thumbnail to open it, tipped the two rings into his palm.

For what seemed an age he stared at them in silence. Then he lifted his head and, a smile lighting his face, reached for her hand and slipped them onto her fourth finger.

'Jared, I want to tell you—'

He rose to his feet and kissed her lips, stopping the words. 'We've talked enough. In the morning there'll be time to say everything else we need to say, to talk about a church wedding with all the trimmings and a honeymoon in Portofino. But for now I just want to make love to you...'

Sweeping her into his arms, he carried her through to the bedroom and, laying her on the bed, sat down on the edge.

When he'd undressed her, taking pleasure in every bare inch of flesh, he stripped off his own clothes and stretched out beside her.

She touched his cheek. 'Won't you let me tell you how very much I love you?'

'I hope you'll tell me every day for the rest of our lives. But just at the moment I'd prefer you to *show* me.'

They made love, and she answered his passion with a passionate tenderness that sent him up in flames and told him everything he needed to know.

When they floated back to earth, their bodies still vibrating with pleasure, he lifted his head from her breast and, having kissed her, said with satisfaction, 'That much, huh.'

* * * * *

Harlequin offers a romance for every mood!
See below for a sneak peek from our
paranormal romance line, Silhouette® Nocturne™.
Enjoy a preview of REUNION by USA TODAY bestselling
author Lindsay McKenna.

Aella closed her eyes and sensed a distinct shift, like
movement from the world around her to the unseen world.

She opened her eyes. And had a slight shock at the man
standing ten feet away. He wasn't just any man. Her heart
leaped and pounded. He reminded her of a fierce warrior
from an ancient civilization. Incan? She wasn't sure but she
felt his deep power and masculinity.

I'm Aella. Are you the guardian of this sacred site? she
asked, hoping her telepathy was strong.

Fox's entire body soared with joy. Fox struggled to put his
personal pleasure aside.

*Greetings, Aella. I'm the assistant guardian to this sacred
area. You may call me Fox. How can I be of service to you,
Aella?* he asked.

*I'm searching for a green sphere. A legend says that the
Emperor Pachacuti had seven emerald spheres created for the
Emerald Key necklace. He had seven of his priestesses and
priests travel the world to hide these spheres from evil forces.
It is said that when all seven spheres are found, restrung and
worn, that Light will return to the Earth. The fourth sphere is
here, at your sacred site. Are you aware of it?* Aella held her
breath. She loved looking at him, especially his sensual
mouth. The desire to kiss him came out of nowhere.

Fox was stunned by the request. *I know of the Emerald Key
necklace because I served the emperor at the time it was*

created. However, I did not realize that one of the spheres is here.

Aella felt sad. Why? Every time she looked at Fox, her heart felt as if it would tear out of her chest. *May I stay in touch with you as I work with this site?* she asked.

Of course. Fox wanted nothing more than to be here with her. To absorb her ephemeral beauty and hear her speak once more.

Aella's spirit lifted. What *was* this strange connection between them? Her curiosity was strong, but she had more pressing matters. In the next few days, Aella knew her life would change forever. How, she had no idea....

Look for REUNION
by USA TODAY *bestselling author Lindsay McKenna,*
available April 2010, only from Silhouette® Nocturne™.

HARLEQUIN *Presents*

2 Stories in 1

HER MEDITERRANEAN PLAYBOY

Sexy and dangerous—he wants you in his bed!

The sky is blue, the azure sea is crashing
against the golden sand and the sun is hot.

The conditions are perfect for
a scorching Mediterranean seduction
from two irresistible untamed playboys!

Indulge your senses with these two delicious stories

A MISTRESS AT THE ITALIAN'S COMMAND
by *Melanie Milburne*

ITALIAN BOSS, HOUSEKEEPER MISTRESS
by *Kate Hewitt*

Available April 2010 from Harlequin Presents!

HARLEQUIN® Romance®

ROMANCE, RIVALRY
AND A FAMILY REUNITED

THE BRIDES
of
BELLA ROSA

William Valentine and his beloved wife, Lucia, live
a beautiful life together, but when his former love Rosa
and the secret family they had together resurface,
an instant rivalry is formed. Can these families
get through the past and come together as one?

*Step into the world of Bella Rosa
beginning this April with*

Beauty and the Reclusive Prince
by
RAYE MORGAN

Eight volumes to collect and treasure!

www.eHarlequin.com

HR17650

LARGER-PRINT BOOKS!

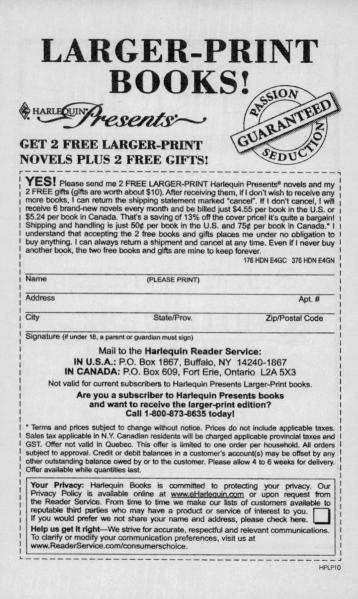

HARLEQUIN *Presents*~

PASSION GUARANTEED SEDUCTION

GET 2 FREE LARGER-PRINT NOVELS PLUS 2 FREE GIFTS!

YES! Please send me 2 FREE LARGER-PRINT Harlequin Presents® novels and my 2 FREE gifts (gifts are worth about $10). After receiving them, if I don't wish to receive any more books, I can return the shipping statement marked "cancel". If I don't cancel, I will receive 6 brand-new novels every month and be billed just $4.55 per book in the U.S. or $5.24 per book in Canada. That's a saving of 13% off the cover price! It's quite a bargain! Shipping and handling is just 50¢ per book in the U.S. and 75¢ per book in Canada.* I understand that accepting the 2 free books and gifts places me under no obligation to buy anything. I can always return a shipment and cancel at any time. Even if I never buy another book, the two free books and gifts are mine to keep forever.

176 HDN E4GC   376 HDN E4GN

Name	(PLEASE PRINT)	
Address		Apt. #
City	State/Prov.	Zip/Postal Code

Signature (if under 18, a parent or guardian must sign)

Mail to the Harlequin Reader Service:
IN U.S.A.: P.O. Box 1867, Buffalo, NY 14240-1867
IN CANADA: P.O. Box 609, Fort Erie, Ontario L2A 5X3

Not valid for current subscribers to Harlequin Presents Larger-Print books.

**Are you a subscriber to Harlequin Presents books
and want to receive the larger-print edition?
Call 1-800-873-8635 today!**

* Terms and prices subject to change without notice. Prices do not include applicable taxes. Sales tax applicable in N.Y. Canadian residents will be charged applicable provincial taxes and GST. Offer not valid in Quebec. This offer is limited to one order per household. All orders subject to approval. Credit or debit balances in a customer's account(s) may be offset by any other outstanding balance owed by or to the customer. Please allow 4 to 6 weeks for delivery. Offer available while quantities last.

Your Privacy: Harlequin Books is committed to protecting your privacy. Our Privacy Policy is available online at www.eHarlequin.com or upon request from the Reader Service. From time to time we make our lists of customers available to reputable third parties who may have a product or service of interest to you. If you would prefer we not share your name and address, please check here. ☐

Help us get it right—We strive for accurate, respectful and relevant communications. To clarify or modify your communication preferences, visit us at www.ReaderService.com/consumerchoice.

HPLP10

▼ *Silhouette*®

SPECIAL EDITION

**INTRODUCING A BRAND-NEW MINISERIES
FROM *USA TODAY* BESTSELLING AUTHOR**

KASEY MICHAELS

SECOND-CHANCE
BRIDAL

At twenty-eight, widowed single mother
Elizabeth Carstairs thinks she's left love behind
forever....until she meets Will Hollingsbrook.
Her sons' new baseball coach is the handsomest
man she's ever seen—and the more time they
spend together, the more undeniable the
connection between them. But can Elizabeth
leave the past behind and open her heart to
a second chance at love?

FIND OUT IN

SUDDENLY A BRIDE

*Available in April
wherever books are sold.*

Visit Silhouette Books at www.eHarlequin.com

SSE65517